UNHEARD VOICES

Collected by
malorie blackman

Also by Malorie Blackman:

The Noughts & Crosses Trilogy
NOUGHTS & CROSSES
KNIFE EDGE
CHECKMATE

A.N.T.I.D.O.T.E.
DANGEROUS REALITY
DEAD GORGEOUS
THE DEADLY DARE MYSTERIES
HACKER
PIG-HEART BOY
THIEF!

www.malorieblackman.co.uk

UNHEARD VOICES

Collected by

malorie
blackman

CORGI

UNHEARD VOICES
A CORGI BOOK 978 0 552 55600 2

Published in Great Britain by Corgi Books,
an imprint of Random House Children's Books

This edition published 2007

7 9 10 8 6

Page ix, Stowage of the British Slave Ship 'Brookes' Under the Regulated Slave Trade Act
of 1788 (engraving) (b/w photo), American School, (18th century)/Library of Congress,
Washington D.C., USA/The Bridgeman Art Library; **Page 3**, The Slave Deck of the Bark
'Wildfire,' Brought into Key West on April 30, 1860, (From a Daguerreotype) Harper's
Weekly. June 2, 1860. 344. Original image public domain, digital scan © Paul
McWhorter/www.sonofthesouth.net; **Page 51**, Slaves. May, 1862 in Cumberland Landing,
Virginia. Original image public domain, digital scan © Paul McWhorter/www.sonofthe-
south.net; **Page 105**, Group of Negroes, as imported to be sold for Slaves, 1793, plate 23
from 'Narrative of a Five Years' Expedition against the Revolted Negroes of Surinam',
engraved by William Blake (1757-1827) pub. 1806 (engraving), Stedman, John Gabriel
(1744-97) (after)/Private Collection, The Stapleton Collection/The Bridgeman Art
Library; **Page 169**, Wedgwood Slave Emancipation Society medallion, c.1787-90
(jasperware) © William Hackwood/The Bridgeman Art Library/Getty Images;
Page 213, Stockbyte/Stockbyte Silver/Getty Images

Set in Times new Roman PS / 11pt

Corgi Books are published by Random House Children's Books,
61–63 Uxbridge Road, London W5 5SA,
a division of The Random House Group Ltd.

Addresses for companies within the Random House Group Limited
can be found at: www.randomhouse.co.uk/offices.htm

THE RANDOM HOUSE GROUP Limited Reg. No. 954009
www.kidsatrandomhouse.co.uk

A CIP catalogue record for this book is available from the British Library.

The Random House Group Limited supports the Forest Stewardship
Council (FSC®), the leading international forest certification organisation.
Our books carrying the FSC label are printed on FSC® certified paper. FSC
is the only forest certification scheme endorsed by the leading environmental
organisations, including Greenpeace. Our paper procurement policy can be
found at www.randomhouse.co.uk/environment

MIX
Paper from
responsible sources
FSC
www.fsc.org
FSC® C013604

Printed and bound by CPI Group (UK) Ltd, Croydon, CR0 4YY

CONTENTS

PART FOUR: TOWARDS FREEDOM

PART FIVE: THE LEGACY OF SLAVERY

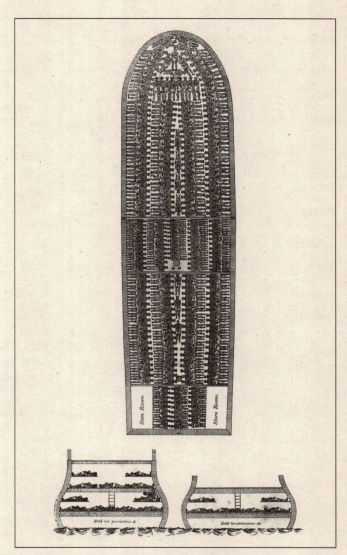

Stowage of the British Slave Ship 'Brookes', 1788

FOREWORD

Welcome to *Unheard Voices*. This is an anthology of stories and poems about slavery written by those who were themselves slaves, as well as by contemporary writers. Why publish such an anthology in the first place? Slavery is an emotive, painful subject that is often shied away from. But more often than not, the only way to move forward is to first look back and learn the lessons of the past. 2007 marks the 200th anniversary of the British Parliament passing the Abolition of the Slave Trade Act 1807. Although the abduction, transportation and selling of slaves didn't stop immediately, it was an important first step.

And unfortunately, even in the twenty-first century, the subject is still relevant. Nowadays, more often than not, it's called 'human trafficking' but it's the same principle – the principle of one human being denying another human being their right to dignity, freedom and equality. Slavery, in all its forms, is a gross abuse of fundamental human rights.

On 10 December 1948 the General Assembly of the

United Nations adopted and proclaimed the Universal Declaration of Human Rights. The Assembly called upon all member countries to publicize the text of the Declaration and 'to cause it to be disseminated, displayed, read and expounded principally in schools and other educational institutions, without distinction based on the political status of countries or territories'.

Article 1 of the Universal Declaration of Human Rights states: 'All human beings are born free and equal in dignity and rights.'

No definition of slavery can adequately convey the full extent of the damage such a trade causes. In addition, many who have been held in slavery or their descendants are subjected to grave abuses of their right to be free from discrimination. One legacy of slavery is perhaps the way in which those descended from slaves, as well as those descended from slave owners or a slave-owning society, view themselves and each other.

Throughout Western history, only a small number of voices have been allowed to tell their story.

Getting published when your voice was outside the perceived 'norm' was all too often a matter of having the right benefactors and patronage. And for too long, slaves were even forbidden to learn to read and write. Education, and thus knowledge, has always been one of the first rights denied to those in slavery.

From my own point of view, although the voyage through my past may make me weep, I can still draw strength from the fact that my ancestors were slaves in the West Indies. Why? Because they survived the inhuman, barbaric transportation from Africa. They survived the inhuman regime they encountered once they reached the West Indies. They survived. I am descended from survivors. And that thought makes me strong.

With this anthology, each writer pays respects to all those men, women and children who made it and somehow survived – and all the many millions who didn't. It is an anthology of work from those to whom the slaves of the past still whisper. Perhaps they will always whisper until slavery and injustice are eliminated from every country on our planet. Let us hope that one day, and soon, that time will come.

Peace.

Malorie Blackman

BENJAMIN ZEPHANIAH

Civil Lies

Dear Teacher,

When I was born in Ethiopia
Life began,
As I sailed down the Nile civilisation began,
When I stopped to think universities were built,
When I set sail
Asians and true Americans sailed with me.

When we traded nations were built,
We did not have animals,
Animals lived with us,
We had so much time

Thirteen months made our year,
We created social services
And cities that still stand.

So Teacher do not say
Columbus discovered me
Check the great things I was doing
Before I suffered slavery.

Yours truly

Mr Africa

PART ONE

CAPTURE AND TRANSPORTATION

JAMES BERRY

Extract from:

Ajeemah and his Son

That wiping out of Atu and Sisi's wedding was always going to be one of the painful happenings.

It was the year 1807. The slave trade was on. By way of that trade, with all its distress, Africans were becoming Caribbean people and Americans. But the sale of Africans as slaves would end. In just another year or so a new British law would stop the British slave trade, and the Americans would soon follow. It would stop Africans being sold to be slaves on plantations in America and the Caribbean.

It was only the importing that would end, not slavery itself, nor the selling of slaves by their existing owners. Stopping the importing was a beginning, and a very welcome start to the end of slavery altogether. Yet even that beginning stirred up wild rage, resistance and awful reactions.

The new law soon to be enforced made people who benefited from the trade all angry, anxious and bitter. The new law made plantation owners cry out. It made them furious at the idea of an end to their regular supply of a free labor force. It caused panic among the ship-owning slave traders and the local African dealers. All ground their teeth in fury and rage at the coming end of their money-making from selling slaves. And the slave traders became determined to work with new vigor. They became determined to beat that end-of-slave-trade deadline, when no more slaves could be shipped; they would get and supply as many more slaves as they could in the short time left.

Remember here too that young people and children came into the slave treatment all the time. They too had to endure a life of no freedom for their parents and for themselves. All was personal for them. The teenage couple Atu and Sisi came into it. They were going to have to face their wedding plans ruined – gone, wiped away as dust.

Truly, European slave buyers would buy. Truly, African traders would obtain their prisoners for sale into slavery. They would find them, even if they had to make their own riots and wars to get prisoners to sell. The slave-trader groups geared and equipped themselves. Their surprise attacks became more unstoppable in the villages. Yet, with all that hidden trouble about, people simply had to go on living their lives.

It was the sunniest of afternoons now. Bird singing filled the day. All unconcerned, Ajeemah and his son Atu walked along their village road in a happy mood. The eighteen-year-old Atu was soon to marry. He and his father were taking a dowry of gold to his expected wife's parents. Going along, not talking, Ajeemah and Atu walked past groups of huts surrounded by bare ground with domestic animals and children playing. They passed fields of yam and grain growing robustly. Atu was thinking about getting married. He knew their coming marriage delighted and excited his sixteen-year-old bride-to-be, Sisi, as much as it did him.

'My father Ajeemah,' Atu said, 'isn't it really something that two other fellows – two others – also wanted to be Sisi's husband?'

Ajeemah didn't look at his son, but a faint smile showed he was amused. 'This bride-gift of gold I carry,' he said, 'will make Sisi's parents receive you well, as a worthy son.'

'I thank you, my father Ajeemah. I know it's your good fatherhood and good heart that make it possible.'

'More than my good heart, it's my thrift. My thrift! You know I'm good at not losing, but keep adding to our wealth.'

'I know, my father, I know. I should have said, may

you continue to have all blessings.'

'And you, my son Atu. May you continue to have all blessings.'

'Thank you, my father Ajeemah.'

'Your mother smiles to herself when she thinks of your coming union with smooth-skinned and bright-eyed Sisi! Good singer, good dancer, that Sunday-born Sisi! Delights everybody!'

'Plays instruments, too.'

'Oh, yes, yes.'

His eyes shining, Atu said, 'She's the best. She pleases everyone.'

'Pleases everyone,' the father agreed.

'And two other fellows shan't get her.'

The father smiled, repeating, 'And two other fellows shan't get her.'

'I'm happy your first wife my mother is happy.'

'Your mother is happy because you'll begin to live your manhood. And she waits for new children you and Sisi will have.'

'And I'm nervous.'

'Nervous?'

'Yes. I'm nervous of all the preparations and ceremonies to get through.'

'That's usual. Marriage makes even a warrior nervous. Especially first marriage.'

'I'll try to enjoy being nervous.'

'Wisdom, wisdom, from a young head!'

'Thank you, my father.'

'Atu, when we get to the house of Sisi's father – Ahta the Twin – watch his face. Watch for the look on his face. First when he thinks I'm empty-handed. Then next when he sees me lift the two pieces of bride-gift gold, one from the inside of each sandal I wear.'

Everybody knew Ajeemah worked in leather and all kinds of skins. In the village he was called 'Skin-man'. He preserved animal, alligator and snake skins and made sandals, bags, belts, bracelets, knife sheaths, ornaments, talismans and pouches for magic charms and spells. But Ajeemah was also known for his practical jokes. He'd chuckled to himself, thinking up the way he'd present Atu's dowry in a most individual and unusual way. He'd created himself the special pair of leather-stringed, lace-up sandals with thick soles. Each sandal had a space under the insole to fit and hide the bride-gift gold in, while he walked to Sisi's house. Ajeemah's big joke was that he'd arrive as if empty-handed. Then, while talking, he'd simply take off each sandal, lift up the insole and produce his gift by surprise. But Atu wasn't at all sold on the idea.

'My father Ajeemah,' Atu said, 'suppose Sisi's father Ahta the Twin is displeased, and things go wrong?'

'True, my son Atu. If Ahta the Twin is displeased, that would be a disaster. But Ahta will not be displeased at all! With the sight of gold for him, Ahta's grin will split his face in two.'

Atu laughed with his father. Won over, Atu now enjoyed his father's scheme along with him. Laughing together, they came around the corner of the footpath, between high bushy banks on each side of the track. And ambushed, with total surprise, Ajeemah and Atu were knocked to the ground, overpowered, by a gang of six Africans with two guns, two dogs, and knives and sticks. With lightning speed, three of their fellow Africans tied Ajeemah's arms behind his back, tightly bandaged his jaws – so he couldn't cry out – and shackled his legs with a chain. The other three tied and shackled Atu the same way. Then, to allow them to see and breathe but not identify, the kidnappers put a bag – a dirty, sickly stinking hood – right down over each captive's head and face.

The kidnappers stood now and stared at the older man. Ajeemah had on more than just a loincloth and his special sandals. Ajeemah wore his magic-spell amulet like a black leather armband. And he wore a flamboyant jacket made of the whole skin of an animal. The front of the jacket was held together with a stringed snakeskin lace; the sides were netted with round and square holes; the back was lengthened with tails of monkeys and lions all round. The leader and his second-in-command both carried the guns. They spoke both the other men's language and

Ajeemah's. The second-in-command said to Ajeemah, 'All dressed up, eh?'

The bushy-bearded leader had thick-set shoulders and short, bulky thighs and arms; he walked with a waddle. Admiring Ajeemah, he took a few steps around him and answered, 'Yeah. Looking like a proper local prince.'

'Ain't he just,' the second-in-command said, undoing Ajeemah's jacket to take it off him. 'This'll do me very nicely!'

'Wait!' the bearded leader warned him. 'Wait! You better watch it!' And he and the others pointed to the magic-spell amulet Ajeemah wore like an armband. 'Take one thing from them,' the gang leader went on, 'and you begin to rot. Every day you wake up a bit more rotten and deformed. A hand falls off. Then another. A leg dries up. An eye closes. Never again to mend. And you're driven raging mad. Haunted, till you just go dumb. Not a word ever again to come.'

Horror, awe and dread blanketed the kidnappers' faces. The hand of the second-in-command fell from

Ajeemah's jacket as if the words he heard paralyzed it. He commanded, 'Get moving!'

Eaten up with rage, with everything in them saying, 'Strike back!' Ajeemah and Atu stood their ground. Blows from a stick rained down on their backs with cutting pain.

'Hold your stick,' the waddling leader said. 'These two are real specials. There's a top price to be demanded for them. We mustn't damage these strong, good-looking bodies.' He signaled the dogs. And growling with menace, the dogs leaped up and gripped the captives as if ready to butcher them till called off. Ajeemah and Atu obeyed and found themselves walking. And with their hands tied, their legs chained, from that moment Ajeemah and Atu would experience treatment they had never believed possible. The kidnappers took Ajeemah and Atu through a wood down to the river. A small boat waited at the bank of the river, guarded by two men with a gun. Four other men and two women were there, shackled and tied together, lying down in the boat.

Ajeemah and Atu had their hoods removed. Made to get into the boat too and lie down, they had their legs tied to the others'. The boat moved off. Ajeemah remembered his gold in a terrible fright, while his ankles were handled. At first he thought he might have lost the gold, then that his guard might have wanted to steal the sandals.

Ah! he said to himself. I still have it! I have Atu's bride-gift gold. I still have on my sandals! That's a good sign. This bride-gift is for my son's bride and goodwill for their children. For nobody else. Nobody else must ever get this gold. I must guard it. Always! . . .

The boat sailed and stopped several times. Sometimes it waited a long time till other captives were brought. Eventually the boat was full.

Night came down. Like all the others with them, Ajeemah and Atu were parched with thirst, empty with hunger and stifled with heat. They were weak. But they were taken from the boat, hands tied and ankles chained. They were made to walk a painful, killing distance in dim lantern light to their overnight stay in hard, bare, prisonlike barracks, where they were given tiny bits of food and very little to drink.

Next day they traveled early and arrived at the coast by dusk. They found themselves taken into a hot, airless, stinking old fort full of other captives. Well guarded, everybody was in some body pain or plain misery. With many hundreds there together, chained up sitting or lying on the floor, the place was a horror of groaning, crying, swearing and noisy gloom. Everybody was in terror over what was going to happen to them.

Next morning, after eating, Ajeemah and Atu found themselves going through the strange business of being oiled up to look clean and shiny for display for sale. In many ways they were lucky. Their trader had put them with a specially selected lot of youthful and strong-looking men, to attract the highest price.

Ajeemah was getting oiled by helpers when the bushy-bearded leader of the kidnappers waddled up, supervising.

'Hello, chiefman!' Ajeemah called. 'Chiefman!'

He looked at Ajeemah. 'What?'

'A word with you.'

His gun hitched up on him, the bulky-limbed, bearded African came close and asked, 'What you want?'

Ajeemah said, 'Where am I going? What's going to happen to me?'

'Don't worry. You won't be eaten.' The kidnapper slave trader said that because of a long-standing belief circulating among captives that white men bought them to eat them.

'Then tell me, how long will I be away?'

'It's up to your buyer to tell you that.'

'I beg you, do a kind favor for me.'

'What's that?'

'Do get a message to my women and children for me. Tell them Ajeemah – Ajeemah and Atu – say we'll be back soon. First chance! First chance we'll be back.'

'Forget it. I don't even know where you come from.'

'Remember where you got me and my

son? Remember? Ask. And get a message to Ahta the Twin – father of my son's bride-to-be. Tell Ahta—'

'Forget it, man. Forget it! I don't know where you come from.'

'I'll tell you. Get a message and I return a good deed for you one day. I come from—'

'Listen. Most I can do for you is to get you in with the best captain I can. D'you hear me?' The slave trader began walking away.

Ajeemah was desperate. He shouted, 'You must do something. You must! My four-year-old son, my son of birth pangs I shared, my Kufuo, must know I'm coming back. He must know!' The slave trader stood and watched his desperate captive. Ajeemah pleaded more quietly. 'My little fellow must know something. No good-byes linger with us. No last tender feeling exchanged – to sustain us! Say you'll get a message – to my family. Please!'

The kidnapper despised Ajeemah for talking like that. He looked at Ajeemah as if he'd just disgraced himself shockingly. 'You've looked like a prince,' he

said, 'and behaved like a warrior, till now.' He waddled away and went on with the supervising of his
slaves being made ready for sale. And standing in
groups, black faces, chests, arms and legs well oiled
and shining, the people were put on show for the
white captains of the waiting ships to come and
choose their purchase.

Ajeemah and Atu had never seen a white man.
They held in their tension and terror and watched
the strange creatures. Ajeemah wondered if his
flesh would end up in the flesh of one of the
white men in captain's hat and high boots.

In a stream of captured people, Ajeemah and
Atu were taken on board ship that same day. Other
slave passengers were already there. By the end
of the day the ship was full of sad, frightened,
grief-stricken and wildly angry people chained
up together. Over three hundred of them, they lay
side by side on fittings like layers of shelves.

When the ship pulled away, noisy weeping and
sobbing broke out. Screams of terror rose up and
ripped through the decks and echoed back to land.

And as the coast of Africa disappeared, a long-drawn-out groan of grief rose up together steadily from the people one after another, till all died away into silence.

Daniel Aloysius Francis

A Day in the Life

**The poem on the next two spreads contrasts two
different viewpoints of the same experience.**

As he looks down at me, and I look up at him.

And I see his white skin,

No differences between me and him,

so he speaks a foreign tongue, we are all unique

but all built the same way.

THUD! I hit the ground; the pain is so loud

When I hit the floor,

I wake up.

I'm home.

The birds are singing, soil between my toes, wind on my hair,

family everywhere, so I just stand and stare.

Nothing's changed and I'm thankful that God made me

This way.

I see my family, so I run to try and greet them,

I'm torn away, I just can't reach them, and every step I take is

dragging me backwards.

The birds stop singing, the soil splashes at my feet, blood in my

hair,

I just don't know where I am.

I wake up, huddled bodies all around me, women screaming, men

chanting, babies crying and

the sound of the majestic sea.
I just don't know where I am,
Am I really here?
Why has God forsaken me and taken away all I hold dear?
Is this the work of Lucifer and his white devils?

Is this my life now huddled deep in the
under world of a distant ship miles from home?

Under the light of the white man's prison I see the squalor
and the sound of salt on open wounds.

It doesn't matter if their skin is white on the surface,
What matters is the evil found underneath!
This is just another average day in the life . . .

* * *

As he looks up at me, and I look down at him.

I look in his eyes and around the face, so I whip his black skin
back until he's unconscious.
Knowing the work I'm doing is righteous.
Delivering the children of God away from sin and savagery,
. . . Into a life of prayer and democracy,
so what if I'm earning a dime a dozen?
Is this not the work of God?
Is this not a deliverance from evil and sin?
Is this not my right to provide for my family doing
the work of God?
So when I die and go to heaven,
I hope I'm rewarded for all this righteous work,
The birds singing, soil between my toes, wind on my face,
family everywhere, a place I can just stand and stare.
Meanwhile I wait for the rewards waiting me in my next life,
transporting all these niggers to the new world,
No matter the murder or strife.

Below deck I hear chanting, of the sinner's world
so I splash more salt on those wide open wounds.

Helping destroy the world of the past and
kill any essence of such savagery,
Why has God blessed me?
Why has Lucifer forgotten about his black devil tongue?
Is this the work of God and those white, white arch angels?

This is my life now delivering sinners from a distant hell,
on this God-given ship, miles from home.
This is just another average day in the life . . .

ALEX HALEY

Extract from:

Roots

Roots *is the story of Kunta Kinte, born in the village of Juffure in The Gambia, West Africa, in the middle of the eighteenth century. When he is seventeen, Kunta is captured by slave catchers while he is looking for wood near his home. He is beaten savagely and when he regains consciousness, Kunta finds himself in a waking nightmare on board a slave ship bound for America . . .*

Kunta wondered if he had gone mad. Naked, chained, shackled, he awoke on his back between two other men in a pitch darkness full of steamy heat and sickening stink and a nightmarish bedlam of shrieking, weeping, praying, and vomiting. He could feel and smell his own vomit on his chest and belly. His whole body was one spasm of pain from the beatings he had received in the four days since his capture. But the place where the hot iron had been put between his shoulders hurt the worst.

A rat's thick, furry body brushed his cheek, its whiskered nose sniffing at his mouth. Quivering with revulsion, Kunta snapped his teeth together desperately, and the rat ran away. In rage, Kunta snatched and kicked against the shackles that bound his wrists and ankles. Instantly, angry exclamations and jerking came back from whomever he was shackled to. The shock and pain adding to his fury, Kunta lunged upward, his head bumping hard against wood – right on the spot where he had been clubbed by the toubob[1] back in the woods. Gasping and snarling, he and the unseen man next to him battered their iron cuffs at each other until both slumped back in exhaustion. Kunta felt himself starting to

[1] A white person.

27

vomit again, and he tried to force it back, but couldn't. His already emptied belly squeezed up a thin, sour fluid that drained from the side of his mouth as he lay wishing that he might die.

He told himself that he mustn't lose control again if he wanted to save his strength and his sanity. After a while, when he felt he could move again, he very slowly and carefully explored his shackled right wrist and ankle with his left hand. They were bleeding. He pulled lightly on the chain; it seemed to be connected to the left ankle and wrist of the man he had fought with. On Kunta's left, chained to him by the ankles, lay some other man, someone who kept up a steady moaning, and they were all so close that their shoulders, arms, and legs touched if any of them moved even a little.

Remembering the wood he had bumped into with his head, Kunta drew himself upward again, just enough for it to bump gently; there wasn't enough space even to sit up. And behind his head was a wooden wall. I'm trapped like a leopard in a snare, he thought. Then he remembered sitting in the darkness of the manhood-training hut after being taken blindfolded to the jujuo so many rains before, and a sob welled up in his throat; but he fought it back. Kunta made himself think about the cries and groans he was hearing all around him. There must be many men here in the blackness, some close, some farther away, some beside him, others in front of him, but all in one room, if that's what this was. Straining his ears, he could hear still more cries, but they were muffled and came from below, beneath the splintery planking he lay on.

Listening more intently, he began to recognize the different tongues of those around him. Over and over, in Arabic, a Fulani was shouting, 'Allah in heaven, help me!' And a man of the Serere tribe was hoarsely wailing what must have been the names of his family. But mostly Kunta heard Mandinkas, the loudest of them babbling wildly in the sira kango secret talk of men, vowing terrible deaths to all toubob. The cries of the others were so slurred with weeping that Kunta could identify neither their words nor their languages, although he knew that some of the strange talk he heard must come from beyond The Gambia.

As Kunta lay listening, he slowly began to realize that he was trying to push from his mind the impulse to relieve the demands of his bowels, which he had been forcing back for days. But he could hold it in no longer, and finally the feces curled out between his buttocks. Revolted at himself, smelling his own addition to the stench, Kunta began sobbing, and again his belly spasmed, producing this time only a little spittle; but he kept gagging. What sins was he being punished for in such a manner as this? He pleaded to Allah for an answer. It was sin enough that he hadn't prayed once since the morning he went for the wood to make his drum. Though he couldn't get onto his knees, and he knew not even which way was east, he closed his eyes where he lay and prayed, beseeching Allah's forgiveness.

Afterward, Kunta lay for a long time bathing dully in his pains, and slowly became aware that one of them, in his knotted stomach, was nothing more than hunger. It occurred to him that he hadn't eaten anything since the night before his capture. He was trying to remember if he had slept in all that time, when suddenly he saw himself walking along a trail in the forest; behind him walked two blacks, ahead of him a pair of toubob with their strange clothes and their long hair in strange colors. Kunta jerked his eyes open and shook his head; he was soaked in sweat and his heart was pounding. He had been asleep without knowing. It had been a nightmare; or was the nightmare this stinking blackness? No, it was as real as the scene in the forest in his dream had been. Against his will, it all came back to him.

After fighting the black slatees[2] and the toubob so desperately in the grove of trees, he remembered awakening – into a wave of blinding pain – and finding himself gagged, blindfolded, and bound with his wrists behind him and his ankles hobbled with knotted rope. Thrashing to break free, he was jabbed savagely with sharp sticks until blood ran down his legs. Yanked onto his feet and prodded with the sticks to begin moving, he stumbled ahead of them as fast as his hobbles would permit.

[2] Slave merchants.

Somewhere along the banks of the bolong – Kunta could tell by the sounds, and the feel of the soft ground beneath his feet – he was shoved down into a canoe. Still blindfolded, he heard the slatees grunting, rowing swiftly, with the toubob hitting him whenever he struggled. Landing, again they walked, until finally that night they reached a place where they threw Kunta on the ground, tied him with his back to a bamboo fence and, without warning, pulled off his blindfold. It was dark, but he could see the pale face of the toubob standing over him, and the silhouettes of others like him on the ground nearby. The toubob held out some meat for him to bite off a piece. He turned his head aside and clamped his jaws. Hissing with rage, the toubob grabbed him by the throat and tried to force his mouth open. When Kunta kept it shut tight, the toubob drew back his fist and punched him hard in the face.

Kunta was let alone the rest of the night. At dawn, he began to make out – tied to other bamboo trunks – the figures of the other captured people, eleven of them – six men, three girls, and two children – all guarded closely by armed slatees and toubob. The girls were naked; Kunta could only avert his eyes; he never had seen a woman naked before. The men, also naked, sat with murderous hatred etched in their faces, grimly silent and crusted with blood from whip cuts. But the girls were crying out, one about dead loved ones in a burned village; another, bitterly weeping, rocked back and forth cooing endearments to an imaginary infant in her cradled arms; and the third shrieked at intervals that she was going to Allah.

In wild fury, Kunta lunged back and forth trying to break his bonds. A heavy blow with a club again knocked him senseless. When he came to, he found that he too was naked, that all of their heads had been shaved and their bodies smeared with red palm oil. At around noonday, two new toubob entered the grove. The slatees, now all grins, quickly untied the captives from the bamboo trunks, shouting to them to stand in a line. Kunta's muscles were knotted with rage and fear. One of the new toubob was short and stout and his hair was white. The other towered over him, tall and huge and scowling, with deep knife scars across his face, but it was the white-haired one before whom the slatees and the other toubob grinned and all but bowed.

Looking at them all, the white-haired one gestured for Kunta to step forward, and lurching backward in terror, Kunta screamed as a whip seared across his back. A slatee from behind grappled him downward to his knees, jerking his head backward. The white-haired toubob calmly spread Kunta's trembling lips and studied his teeth. Kunta attempted to spring up, but after another blow of the whip, he stood as ordered, his body quivering as the toubob's fingers explored his eyes, his chest, his belly. When the fingers grasped his foto, he lunged aside with a choked cry. Two slatees and more lashings were needed to force Kunta to bend over almost double, and in horror he felt his buttocks being spread wide apart. Then the white-haired toubob roughly shoved Kunta aside and, one by one, he similarly inspected the others, even the private parts of the wailing girls. Then whips and shouted commands sent the captives all dashing around within the enclosure, and next springing up and down on their haunches.

After observing them, the white-haired toubob and the huge one with the knife-scarred face stepped a little distance away and spoke briefly in low tones. Stepping back, the white-haired one, beckoning another toubob, jabbed his finger at four men, one of them Kunta, and two of the girls. The toubob looked shocked, pointing at the others in a beseeching manner. But the white-haired one shook his head firmly. Kunta sat straining against his bonds, his head threatening to burst with rage, as the toubob argued heatedly. After a while, the white-haired one disgustedly wrote something on a piece of paper that the other toubob angrily accepted.

Kunta struggled and howled with fury as the slatees grabbed him again, wrestling him to a seated position with his back arched. Eyes wide with terror, he watched as a toubob withdrew from the fire a long, thin iron that the white-haired one had brought with him. Kunta was already thrashing and screaming as the iron exploded pain between his shoulders. The bamboo grove echoed with the screams of the others, one by one. Then red palm oil was rubbed over the peculiar LL shape Kunta saw on their backs.

Within the hour, they were hobbling in a line of clanking chains, with the slatees' ready whips flailing down on anyone who balked or stumbled. Kunta's back and shoulders were ribboned with bleeding cuts when late that night they reached two canoes hidden under thick, overhanging mangroves at the river's banks. Split into two groups, they were rowed through darkness by the slatees, with the toubob lashing out at any sign of struggle.

When Kunta saw a vast dark shape looming up ahead in the night, he sensed that this was his last chance. Springing and lunging amid shouts and screams around him, he almost upset the canoe in his struggle to leap overboard; but he was bound to the others and couldn't make it over the side. He almost didn't feel the blows of the whips and clubs against his ribs, his back, his face, his belly, his head – as the canoe bumped against the side of the great dark thing. Through the pain, he could feel the warm blood pouring down his face, and he heard above him the exclamations of many toubob. Then ropes were being looped around him, and he was helpless to resist. After being half pushed and half pulled up some strange rope ladder, he had enough strength left to twist his body wildly in another break for freedom; again he was lashed with whips, and hands were grabbing him amid an overwhelming toubob smell and the sound of women shrieking and loud toubob cursing.

Through swollen lids, Kunta saw a thicket of legs and feet all around him, and managing an upward glance while trying to shield his bleeding face with his forearm, he saw the short toubob with the white hair standing calmly making marks in a small book with a stubby pencil. Then he felt himself being snatched upright and shoved roughly across a flat space. He caught a glimpse of tall poles with thick wrappings of coarse white cloth. Then he was being guided, stumbling weakly down some kind of narrow steps, into a place of pitch blackness;

at the same instant, his nose was assaulted by an unbelievable stink, and his ears by cries of anguish.

Kunta began vomiting as the toubob – holding dim yellowish flames that burned within metal frames carried by a ring – shackled his wrists and ankles, then shoved him backward, close between two other moaning men. Even in his terror, he sensed that lights bobbing in other directions meant that the toubob were taking those who had come with him to be shackled elsewhere. Then he felt his thoughts slipping; he thought he must be dreaming. And then, mercifully, he was.

* * *

Only the rasping sound of the deck hatch being opened told Kunta if it was day or night. Hearing the latch click, he would jerk his head up – the only free movement that his chains and shackles would allow – and four shadowy toubob figures would descend, two of them with bobbing lights and whips guarding the other pair as they all moved along the narrow aisleways pushing a tub of food. They would thrust tin pans of the stuff up onto the filth between each two shacklemates. So far, each time the food had come, Kunta had clamped his jaws shut, preferring to starve to death, until the aching of his empty stomach had begun to make his hunger almost as terrible as the pains from his beatings. When those on Kunta's level had been fed, the lights showed the toubob descending farther below with the rest of the food.

Less often than the feeding times, and usually when it was night outside, the toubob would bring down into the hold some new captives, screaming and whimpering in terror as they were shoved and lashed along to wherever they were to be chained into empty spaces along the rows of hard plank shelves.

One day, shortly after a feeding time, Kunta's ears picked up a strange, muted sound that seemed to vibrate through the ceiling over his head. Some of the other men heard it too, and their moaning ended abruptly. Kunta lay listening intently; it sounded as if many feet were dashing about overhead. Then – much nearer to them in the darkness – came a new sound, as of some very heavy object being creaked very slowly upward.

Kunta's naked back felt an odd vibration from the hard, rough planking he lay on. He felt a tightening, a swelling within his chest, and he lay frozenly. About him he heard thudding sounds that he knew were men lunging upward, straining against their chains. It felt as if all of his blood had rushed into his pounding head. And then terror went clawing into his vitals as he sensed in some way that this place was moving, taking them away. Men started shouting all around him, screaming to Allah and His spirits, banging their heads against the planking, thrashing wildly against their rattling shackles. 'Allah, I will never pray to you less than five times daily!' Kunta shrieked into the bedlam. 'Hear me! Help me!'

The anguished cries, weeping, and prayers continued, subsiding only as one after another exhausted man went limp and lay gasping for breath in the stinking blackness. Kunta knew that he would never see Africa again. He could feel clearly now, through his body against the planks, a slow, rocking motion, sometimes enough that his shoulders or arms or hips would press against the brief warmth of one of the men he was chained between. He had shouted so hard that he had no voice left, so his mind screamed it instead: 'Kill toubob – and their traitor black helpers!'

He was sobbing quietly when the hatch opened and the four toubob came bumping down with their tub of food. Again he clamped his jaws against his spasms of hunger, but then he thought of something the kintango had once said – that warriors and hunters must eat well to have greater strength than other men. Starving himself meant that weakness would prevent him from killing toubob. So this time, when the pan was thrust onto the boards between him and the man next to him, Kunta's fingers also clawed into the thick mush. It tasted like ground maize boiled with palm oil. Each gulping swallow pained his throat in the spot where he had been choked for not eating before, but he swallowed until the pan was empty. He could feel the food like a lump in his belly, and soon it was rising up his throat. He couldn't stop it, and a moment later the gruel was back on the planking. He could hear, over the sound of his own retching, that of others doing the same thing.

As the lights approached the end of the long shelf of planks on which Kunta lay, suddenly he heard chains rattling, a head bumping, and then a man screaming hysterically in a curious mixture of Mandinka and what sounded like some toubob words. An uproarious burst of laughter came from the toubob with the feeding tub, then their whips lashing down, until the man's cries lapsed, into babbling and whimpering. Could it be? Had he heard an African speaking toubob? Was there slatee down there among them? Kunta had heard that toubob would often betray their black traitor helpers and throw them into chains.

After the toubob had gone on down to the level below, scarcely a sound was heard on Kunta's level until they reappeared with their emptied tub and climbed back up outside, closing the hatch behind them. At that instant, an angry buzzing began in different tongues, like bees swarming. Then, down the shelf from where Kunta lay, there was a heavy chain-rattling blow, a howl of pain and bitter cursing in the same hysterical Mandinka. Kunta heard the man shriek, 'You think I am toubob?' There were more violent, rapid blows and desperate screams. Then the blows stopped, and in the blackness of the hold came a high squealing – and then an awful gurgling sound, as of a man whose breath was being choked off. Another rattling of chains, a tattoo of bare heels kicking at the planks, then quiet.

Kunta's head was throbbing, and his heart was pounding, as voices around him began screaming, 'Slatee! Slatees die!' Then Kunta was screaming along with them and joining in a wild rattling of chains – when suddenly with a rasping sound the hatch was opened, admitting its shaft of daylight and a group of toubob with lights and whips. They had obviously heard the commotion below them, and though now almost total silence had fallen in the hold, the toubob rushed among the aisles shouting and lashing left and right with their whips. When they left without finding the dead man, the hold remained silent for a long moment. Then, very quietly, Kunta heard a mirthless laugh from the end of the shelf next to where the traitor lay dead.

The next feeding was a tense one. As if the toubob sensed something amiss, their whips fell even more often than usual. Kunta jerked and cried out as a bolt of pain cut across his legs. He had learned that when anyone didn't cry out from a blow, he would get a severe beating until he did. Then he clawed and gulped down the tasteless mush as his eyes followed the lights moving on down along the shelf.

Every man in the hold was listening when one of the toubob exclaimed something to the others. A jostling of lights could be seen, then more exclamations and cursings, and then one of the toubob rushed down the aisle and up through the hatch, and he soon returned with two more. Kunta could hear the iron cuffs and chains being unlocked. Two of the toubob then half carried, half dragged the body of the dead man along the aisle and up the hatch, while the others continued bumping their food tub along the aisles.

The food team was on the level below when four more toubob climbed down through the hatch and went directly to where the slatee had been chained. By twisting his head, Kunta could see the lights raised high. With violent cursing, two of the toubob sent their whips whistling down against flesh. Whoever was being beaten refused at first to scream; though just listening to the force of the blows was almost paralyzing to Kunta, he could hear the beaten man flailing against his chains in the agony of his torture – and of his grim determination not to cry out.

Then the toubob were almost shrieking their curses, and the lights could be seen changing hands as one man spelled the other with the lash. Finally the beaten man began screaming – first a Foulah curse, then things that could not be understood, though they too were in the Foulah tongue. Kunta's mind flashed a thought of the quiet, gentle Foulah tribe who tended Mandinka cattle – as the lashing sounds continued until the beaten man barely whimpered. Then the four toubob left, cursing, gasping, and gagging in the stink.

The moans of the Foulah shivered through the black hold. Then, after a while, a clear voice called out in Mandinka, 'Share his pain! We must be in this place as one village!' The voice belonged to an elder. He was right. The Foulah's pains had been as Kunta's own. He felt himself about to burst with rage. He also felt, in some nameless way, a terror greater than he had ever known before, and it seemed to spread from the marrow of his bones. Part of him wanted to die, to escape all of this; but no, he must live to avenge it. He forced himself to lie absolutely still. It took a long while, but finally he felt his strain and confusion, even his body's pains, begin to ebb – except for the place between his shoulders where he had been burned with the hot iron. He found that his mind could focus better now on the only choice that seemed to lie before him and the others: Either they would all die in this nightmare place, or somehow the toubob would have to be overcome and killed.

Roots *is the result of Alex Haley's search for his family's origins. It took him over ten years of research to trace his family tree back to Kunta Kinte, who was sixteen years old when he was snatched from his home in The Gambia, West Africa, and transported to America to be sold as a slave. Before he wrote about the horrific journey in the slave-ship hold, Alex Haley booked a place on a freighter travelling from Africa to America. Each night after dinner, he climbed into the deep, cold cargo hold and, wearing only his underwear, lay on his back on a plank and forced himself to stay there for the duration of the night, trying to imagine what Kunta Kinte would have seen, smelled, tasted and thought during the horrendous voyage.*

JOHN AGARD

Newton's Amazing Grace

*(John Newton [1725-1807], slave-ship captain, who
converted to the ministry and composed many hymns,
including 'Amazing Grace'.)*

Grace is not a word for which I had much use.
And I skippered ships that did more than bruise
the face of the Atlantic. I carved my name
in human cargo without a thought of shame.
But the sea's big enough for a man to lose
his conscience, if not his puny neck.
In the sea's eye, who is this upstart speck
that calls himself a maker of history?
It took a storm to save the dumb wretch in me.

On a night the winds weighed heavy as my sins,
I spared a thought for those poor souls below deck.
Terror made rough waters my Damascus road.
Amazing grace began to lead me home.
Lord, let my soul's scum be measured by a hymn.

PART TWO

THE LIFE OF A SLAVE

FREDERICK DOUGLASS

Extract from:

The Narrative of the Life of Frederick Douglass, an American Slave

---

Frederick Douglass was born into slavery in the state of Maryland sometime in the year of 1818. His exact birthday was never recorded. He was taken away from his mother at a very young age and never knew who his father was, although it was suspected it may have been his white master. When his first owner died, Frederick was sent to Baltimore, where the wife of his new master taught him the alphabet. He continued to learn to read from the white children in the neighbourhood. In 1838 Frederick escaped slavery by boarding a train dressed as a seaman and travelling to New York. His autobiography was published in 1845 and some critics thought that it wasn't possible for an ex-slave to write so eloquently but the book became a bestseller. As well as writing about his life, Frederick gave lectures, wrote essays and published a series of newspapers in collaboration with the anti-slavery movement, becoming one of the most powerful and influential black Americans of his time.

I was born in Tuckahoe, near Hillsborough, and about twelve miles from Easton, in Talbot county, Maryland. I have no accurate knowledge of my age, never having seen any authentic record containing it. By far the larger part of the slaves know as little of their ages as horses know of theirs, and it is the wish of most masters within my knowledge to keep their slaves thus ignorant. I do not remember to have ever met a slave who could tell of his birthday. They seldom come nearer to it than planting-time, harvest-time, cherry-time, spring-time, or fall-time. A want of information concerning my own was a source of unhappiness to me even during childhood. The white children could tell their ages. I could not tell why I ought to be deprived of the same privilege. I was not allowed to make any inquiries of my master concerning it. He deemed all such inquiries on the part of a slave improper and impertinent, and evidence of a restless spirit. The nearest estimate I can give makes me now between twenty-seven and twenty-eight years of age. I come to this, from hearing my master say, some time during 1835, I was about seventeen years old.

My mother was named Harriet Bailey. She was the daughter of Isaac and Betsey Bailey, both colored, and quite dark. My mother was of a darker complexion than either my grandmother or grandfather.

My father was a white man. He was admitted to be such by all I ever heard speak of my parentage. The opinion was also whispered that my master was my father; but of the correctness of this opinion, I know nothing; the means of knowing was withheld from me. My mother and I were separated when I was but an infant – before I knew her as my mother. It is a common custom, in the part of Maryland from which I ran away, to part children from their mothers at a very early age. Frequently, before the child has reached its twelfth month, its mother is taken from it, and hired out on some farm a considerable distance off, and the child is placed under the care of an old woman, too old for field labor. For what this separation is done, I do not know, unless it be to hinder the development of the child's affection toward its mother, and to blunt and destroy the natural affection of the mother for the child. This is the inevitable result.

I never saw my mother, to know her as such, more than four or five times in my life; and each of these times was very short in duration, and at night. She was hired by a Mr Stewart, who lived about twelve miles from my home. She made her journeys to see me in the night, travelling the whole distance on foot, after the performance of her day's work. She was a field hand, and a whipping is the penalty of not being in the field at sunrise, unless a slave has special permission from his or her master to the contrary – a permission which they seldom get, and one that gives to him that gives it the proud name of being a kind master. I do not recollect of ever seeing my mother by the light of day. She was with me in the night. She would lie down with me, and get me to sleep, but long before I waked she was gone. Very little communication ever took place between us. Death soon ended what little we could have while she lived, and with it her hardships and suffering. She died when I was about seven years old, on one of my master's farms, near Lee's Mill. I was not allowed to be present during her illness, at her death, or burial. She was gone long before I knew any thing about it. Never having enjoyed, to any considerable extent, her soothing presence, her tender and watchful care, I received the tidings of her death with much the same emotions I should have probably felt at the death of a stranger.

Frederick Douglass: 1817–1895

Douglass was someone who,
Had he walked with wary foot
And frightened tread,
From very indecision
Might be dead,
Might have lost his soul,
But instead decided to be bold
And capture every street
On which he set his feet,
To route each path
Toward freedom's goal,
To make each highway
Choose *his* compass' choice,

To all the world cried,
Hear my voice! . . .
Oh, to be a beast, a bird,
Anything but a slave! he said.

Who would be free
Themselves must strike
The first blow, he said.

He died in 1895.
He is not dead.

MARY PRINCE

Extracts from:

The History of Mary Prince, a West Indian Slave

Mary Prince was born a slave in Bermuda, the West Indies, probably in the year 1788. She was sold several times to different masters, travelling to Grand Turks and Antigua, where she fell in love with, and married, a former slave, Daniel Jones, who had bought his freedom. When her master found out she had married, she was severely beaten. In 1828 she was taken by her master to London. Slavery was illegal in Britain but Mary had no means of supporting herself. Eventually, however, after being thrown out by her master, she found employment with Thomas Pringle, a leading figure in the British anti-slavery movement. Pringle arranged for Mary's story to be written down and it was published in 1831, making Mary the first woman to publish the story of her slavery.

These extracts describe how Mary was sold away from her mother and sisters and the cruelty she and a fellow slave experienced at the hands of their owner.

The black morning at length came; it came too soon for my poor mother and us. Whilst she was putting on us the new osnaburgs[1] in which we were to be sold, she said, in a sorrowful voice, (I shall never forget it!) 'See, I am *shrouding* my poor children; what a task for a mother!' – She then called Miss Betsey to take leave of us. 'I am going to carry my little chickens to market,' (these were her very words), 'take your last look of them; may be you will see them no more.' 'Oh, my poor slaves! my own slaves!' said dear Miss Betsey, 'you belong to me; and it grieves my heart to part with you.' – Miss Betsey kissed us

---

[1] Clothes made from coarse plain-woven cotton.

all, and, when she left us, my mother called the rest of the slaves to bid us good bye. One of them, a woman named Moll, came with her infant in her arms. 'Ay!' said my mother, seeing her turn away and look at her child with the tears in her eyes, 'your turn will come next.' The slaves could say nothing to comfort us; they could only weep and lament with us. When I left my dear little brothers and the house in which I had been brought up, I thought my heart would burst.

Our mother, weeping as she went, called me away with the children Hannah and Dinah, and we took the road that led to Hamble Town, which we reached about four o'clock in the afternoon. We followed my mother to the marketplace, where she placed us in a row against a large house, with our backs to the wall and our arms folded across our breasts. I, as the eldest, stood first, Hannah next to me, then Dinah; and our mother stood beside crying over us. My heart throbbed with grief and terror so violently, that I pressed my hands quite tightly across my breast, but I could not keep it still, and it continued to leap as though it would burst out of my body. But who cared for that? Did one of the many by-standers, who were looking at us so carelessly, think of the pain that wrung the hearts of the negro woman and her young ones? No, no! They were not all bad, I dare say, but slavery hardens white people's hearts towards the blacks; and many of them were not slow to make their remarks upon us aloud, without regard to our grief – though their light words fell like cayenne on the fresh wounds of our hearts. Oh those white people have small hearts who can only feel for themselves.

At length the vendue master, who was to offer us for sale like sheep or cattle, arrived, and asked my mother which was the eldest. She said nothing, but pointed to me. He took me by the hand, and led me out into the middle of the street, and, turning me slowly round, exposed me to the view of those who attended the vendue. I was soon surrounded by strange men, who examined and handled me in the same manner that a butcher would a calf or a lamb he was about to purchase, and who talked about my shape and size in like words – as if I could no more understand their meaning than the dumb beasts. I was then put up to sale. The bidding commenced at a few pounds, and gradually rose to fifty-seven, when I was knocked down to the highest bidder; and the people who stood by said that I had fetched a great sum for so young a slave.

I then saw my sisters led forth, and sold to different owners; so that we had not the sad satisfaction of being partners in bondage. When the sale was over, my mother hugged and kissed us, and mourned over us, begging of us to keep up a good heart, and do our duty to our new masters. It was a sad parting; one went one way, one another, and our poor mammy went home with nothing.

* * *

Poor Hetty, my fellow slave, was very kind to me, and I used to call her my Aunt; but she led a most miserable life, and her death was hastened (at least the slaves all believed and said so), by the dreadful chastisement she received from my master during her pregnancy. It happened as follows. One of the cows had dragged the rope away from the stake to which Hetty had fastened it, and got loose. My master flew into a terrible passion, and ordered the poor creature to be stripped quite naked, notwithstanding her pregnancy, and to be tied up to a tree in the yard. He then flogged her as hard as he could lick, both with the whip and cow-skin, till she was all over streaming with blood. He rested, and then beat her again and again. Her shrieks were terrible. The consequence was that poor Hetty was brought to bed before her time, and was delivered after severe labour of a dead child. She appeared to recover after her confinement, so far that she was repeatedly flogged by both master and mistress afterwards; but her former strength never returned to her. Ere long her body and limbs swelled to a great size; and she lay on a mat in the kitchen, till the water burst out of her body and she died. All the slaves said that death was a good thing for poor Hetty; but I cried very much for her death.

The manner of it filled me with horror. I could not bear to think about it; yet it was always present to my mind for many a day.

After Hetty died all her labours fell upon me, in addition to my own. I had now to milk eleven cows every morning before sunrise, sitting among the damp weeds; to take care of the cattle as well as the children; and to do the work of the house. There was no end to my toils – no end to my blows. I lay down at night and rose up in the morning in fear and sorrow; and often wished that like poor Hetty I could escape from this cruel bondage and be at rest in the grave. But the hand of God whom then I knew not, was stretched over me; and I was mercifully preserved for better things. It was then, however, my heavy lot to weep, weep, weep, and that for years; to pass from one misery to another, and from one cruel master to a worse. But I must go on with the thread of my story.

One day a heavy squall of wind and rain came on suddenly, and my mistress sent me round the corner of the house to empty a large earthen jar. The jar was already cracked with an old deep crack that divided it in the middle, and in turning it upside down to empty it, it parted in my hand. I could not help the accident, but I was dreadfully frightened, looking forward to a severe punishment. I ran crying to my mistress, 'O mistress, the jar has come in two.' 'You have broken it, have you?' she replied; 'come directly here to me.' I came trembling; she stripped and flogged me long and severely with the cow-skin; as long as she had strength to use the lash, for she did not give over till she was quite tired. – When my master came home at night, she told him of my fault; and oh, frightful! how he fell a swearing. After abusing me with every ill name he could think of, (too, too bad to speak in England,) and giving me several heavy blows with his hand, he said, 'I shall come home to-morrow morning at twelve, on purpose to give you a round hundred.' He kept his word – Oh sad for me! I cannot easily forget it. He tied me up upon a ladder, and gave me a hundred lashes with his own hand, and master Benjy stood by to count them for him. When he had licked me for some time he sat down to take breath; then after resting, he beat me again and again, until he was quite wearied, and so hot (for the weather was very sultry), that he sank back in his chair, almost like to faint. While my mistress went to bring him a drink, there was a dreadful earthquake. Part of the roof fell down, and every thing in the house went – clatter, clatter, clatter. Oh I thought the end of all things near at hand; and I was so sore with the flogging, that I scarcely cared whether I lived or died. The earth was groaning and shaking; every thing tumbling about; and my mistress and the slaves were shrieking and crying out, 'The earthquake! the earthquake!' It was an awful day for us all.

During the confusion I crawled away on my hands and knees, and laid myself down under the steps of the piazza, in front of the house. I was in a dreadful state – my body all blood and bruises, and I could not help moaning piteously. The other slaves, when they saw me, shook their heads and said, 'Poor child! poor child!' – I lay there till the morning, careless of what might happen, for life was very weak in me, and I wished more than ever to die. But when we are very young, death always seems a great way off, and it would not come that night to me. The next morning I was forced by my master to rise and go about my usual work, though my body and limbs were so stiff and sore, that I could not move without the greatest pain. – Nevertheless, even after all this severe punishment, I never heard the last of that jar; my mistress was always throwing it in my face.

Some little time after this, one of the cows got loose from the stake, and eat one of the sweet-potatoe slips. I was milking when my master found it out. He came to me, and without any more ado, stooped down, and taking off his heavy boot, he struck me such a severe blow in the small of my back, that I shrieked with agony, and thought I was killed; and I feel a weakness in that part to this day. The cow was frightened at his violence, and kicked down the pail and spilt the milk all about. My master knew that this accident was his own fault, but he was so enraged that he seemed glad of an excuse to go on with his ill usage. I cannot remember how many licks he gave me then, but he beat me till I was unable to stand, and till he himself was weary.

After this I ran away and went to my mother, who was living with Mr Richard Darrel. My poor mother was both grieved and glad to see me; grieved because I had been so ill used, and glad because she had not seen me for a long, long while. She dared not receive me into the house, but she hid me up in a hole in the rocks near, and brought me food at night, after every body was asleep. My father, who lived at Crow-Lane, over the salt-water channel, at last heard of my being hid up in the cavern, and he came and took me back to my master. Oh I was loth, loth to go back; but as there was no remedy, I was obliged to submit.

LALITA TADEMY

Extract from:

Cane River

Cane River *is based on the history of the author's ancestors.*

Suzette is a slave, born on a medium-sized Creole plantation in central Louisiana. The youngest daughter in a family of four children, she works in the big house where her mother is the cook. But as Suzette reaches thirteen years of age, her life is changed for ever.

Christmas Day was dry and chilly. The crop had been

a good one this year, in a succession of very good years, and the talk of the quarter for the prior two weeks had turned to what the gifts would likely be. It was certain that there would be the big contest for the best cuts of beef, and one bottle of liquor for each man, and new blankets, but they couldn't guess the surprise. They speculated that whatever it was would be store-bought since no one from the house or the field had had a hand in its preparation. Maybe broadcloth for new trousers or seed for their gardens.

The week between Christmas and New Year's would pass without any heavy fieldwork. Only music and food, singing, dancing, and drinking. Visiting, fishing, courting, and sleeping-in until after the sun was already up. Friends and family gathering in the light of daytime. Mothers nursing their babies according to the baby's need instead of the plantation bell. Traveling to other plantations to see family. The luxury of planning. Planning the flow of each day for one full week.

No cotton would be planted, hoed, or picked. When the plantation bell sounded, it would mark the passage of time, but it would not begin the march to the north field before sunrise. No backs stooped over this week except to work a personal patch or bend over a checkerboard. No long sack hung around the neck to drag between endless rows of cotton plants. No weighing of each basket at twilight to measure performance against quota. No bold script recording one hundred and seventy-five pounds next to the name *Palmire* in the big plantation book. Two hundred and three for Gerasíme. Forty-six for Solataire, just starting out at the age of eleven as a one-quarter hand.

Suzette wiped her forehead with the back of her sleeve while she threw pine chips into the cookhouse fireplace. The flames spat and burned hotter.

'Christmas morning, and we're the only ones working,' she grumbled under her breath.

'Don't try to match up one misery against another,' Elisabeth said. 'Field or house, we're all in the same web, waiting for the spider to get home.'

Elisabeth never broke her rhythm as she stirred the batter for griddle cakes. She had spent the night down in the quarter with Gerasíme and was in a very good mood. 'Besides, that's no talk for Christmas,' she went on. 'This is the Lord's day.'

If Suzette was cheerful, her mother's response was likely to be full of gloom. If Suzette was sulky, it would be something full of false hope and cheer. But even as she was complaining, Suzette's heart wasn't really in it. Tonight was the big quarter Christmas party at Rosedew.

Some of the slaves owned by their smaller neighbors would be coming, including the three from François Mulon's farm. Suzette wished that Nicolas would come, but the *gens de couleur libre* kept to their own for social occasions. It seemed to Suzette that Nicolas saved his smiles for her since their communion classes, and she certainly saved her thoughts for him. She still kept the scrap of cowhide he had given her close at hand, most times in her apron pocket or hidden beneath her pallet. Nicolas had dreams, planning to have his own place along Cane River by hiring himself out. But Nicolas or no, Suzette intended to have fun tonight.

Only thirteen, Suzette had already sold some of her

baking along Cane River. She had even been rented out once to the Rachal place for one of their big parties. She sometimes sneaked her cooking to her family, but tonight they could enjoy their treats out in the open, without the risk of being caught.

Determined to make this Christmas feast the best yet on Rosedew, she and Elisabeth had been cooking for days. They would serve up portions for the Derbannes separately, but the rest was for the tables that had been set up in the barn, where the entire quarter would gather. On Christmas Day everyone could have as much to eat as they wanted.

Suzette did a few sample steps of the waltz with an elaborate dip at the end in her mother's direction. Elisabeth laughed, and peace was restored.

'Can I wear my first communion dress for the party?' Suzette asked.

'I hope it still fits,' Elisabeth said. 'You're growing more curves every day.'

'I heard M'sieu Louis talking to M'sieu Eugene Daurat,' Suzette said. 'He said the week off between Christmas and New Year's is just a way to make the hands more manageable the rest of the year. To let them blow off steam so they don't get ideas about running.'

'Let *us* blow off steam,' Elisabeth corrected. 'We're all in the same web.'

'Anyway, he invited M'sieu Eugene to come to the big contest.'

'Suzette, I want you to stay away from that little man as much as you can. Try not to be alone with him.'

'He means no harm, *Mère.*'

'The man already struts around this place like he owns it. Like everything here is his for the taking. Tell me you'll take care.'

Eugene had been nice to Suzette, always had an easy smile for her.

'Yes, *Mère.*'

'We're ready,' Elisabeth said, making one last inspection of the griddle. 'Let's go on up to the house.'

There was a small crowd from the quarter outside

of the big house. Gerasíme, hair wild and eyes alert, drew his jacket tighter around his body against the chill. He had chosen a place nearest the front door to stand, and his children, Palmire, Apphia, and Solataire, flanked him. Suzette and Elisabeth headed toward them.

'First light come and gone,' Gerasíme said when he saw Elisabeth. 'They're starting late.'

As if on cue, Louis, Françoise, and Oreline came out onto the front gallery still in their nightclothes. Louis rubbed his eyes and yawned.

'What are you all doing here?' he asked gruffly.

'Christmas gifts,' they shouted back in one voice.

'Surely it isn't Christmas already?'

Gerasíme spoke up. 'M'sieu, it surely is.'

Louis looked doubtful and slowly drew his fingers through his hair.

'I may have something I could find to give,' he said at last, and with a great flourish he drew the cover off the makeshift table set up against the front of the house.

Underneath were forty-eight Christmas stockings,

each filled with nuts, oranges, apples, pecan candy, and a ten-hole harmonica for each hand over the age of five. As they came forward to receive their stocking, Louis greeted each by name. All men got a jug of whiskey, each woman a length of muslin and gabardine, and everyone received their new blanket for the year.

Suzette and Elisabeth slipped away while Louis was still handing out gifts and began to serve up the breakfast of scrambled eggs, smoked ham, flapjacks with cane syrup, and café noir. There was to be an uninterrupted flow of food of every description all day long, and it would be considered a sad failure if anyone left the tables hungry.

By the time Louis, Françoise, Oreline, and Eugene Daurat made their appearance at the annual celebration in the quarter, dressed in their finery, the party had been going for some time. By custom they knew not to stay too long. Heaping platters of meat, vegetables, breads, and sweets were arranged on makeshift tables. Gumbo waited in the heavy black kettle steaming over an open fire. Old Bertram carved pieces from the crackling porker barbecuing in a deep pit.

'Time for the big contest,' Louis announced, leading the way to one side of the barn. 'Who's first?'

'Old Bertram's the oldest,' came the shout back.

They cleared a path, and Old Bertram came forward. Louis handed him a bow and arrow.

Outlined on the side of the barn in charcoal was the crudely drawn picture of a cow, and Old Bertram drew back the arrow and let it fly. The point made a soft *thunk*, landing near the top of the cow image's tail.

'Looks like Old Bertram gets tail stew,' Gerasíme said, laughing.

'I call that close enough for rump roast,' Louis said.

Old Bertram looked very pleased with himself. He would get to keep a piece of the meat from that section of the cow to be slaughtered the next day.

'See if you can do better,' Old Bertram sniffed, giving up the bow and arrow to Gerasíme.

Gerasíme took aim, and his arrow tip landed squarely in the center.

'Short loin!' Louis called out, and the crowd whistled and cheered.

Some of the men had gotten such a head start on the whiskey, they had trouble hitting the target at all on the first try.

After the big contest, Gerasíme picked up his fiddle and the dancing began. Suzette watched her mother with delight. Elisabeth danced in the clearing with the others, her good lace scarf pulled across her shoulders and tied neatly in front of her ample chest, first flying up and then falling down with each movement. Eyes wide and full of spirit, she picked up her long skirt to give her feet more maneuvering room, looking at her partners but more often over at Gerasíme, playing his fiddle under the oak tree. Elisabeth smiled and winked at Gerasíme, broadly, in front of the entire quarter, in front of the Derbannes and their guests, and Gerasíme winked back.

Suzette found herself responding to the gaiety of

the music, finally getting her chance to dance. She pulled first one and then another into the center of the dance floor, teaching anyone who didn't know the steps and wanted to learn. She danced the quadrille waltz and the *fais do do*, while her father played the fiddle. The *fais do do* was her favorite, with six couples taking the lead from Gerasíme as he called the figures in French faster and faster in a contest between dancer and musician.

The dancers leaned on one another in exhaustion when the number was over, laughing and panting, hearts racing, adrenaline left over. Suzette closed her eyes, and she could see herself in her white dress in the chapel at St Augustine with Nicolas beside her. When she opened her eyes, Eugene Daurat was staring at her fixedly, familiarity in his gaze, as if there were some secret between them. Suzette pulled her eyes away from his, her confusion laced with a trace of shame, although she knew she had done nothing wrong. The music started up again, and her little brother, Solataire, tugged at her hand to dance.

After the set finished she decided to take herself

away from the noise and closeness for a moment. The party would go on until almost dawn.

'You are a wonderful partner, brother,' she said to Solataire with a fond smile. 'I am counting on another dance as soon as I return.' She had not felt so free since she was a child.

It was a crisp December evening, cold enough for Suzette to see traces of her own breath on the frosty air, but she had worked up a sweat. She headed off dreamily through the woods to cool off and to think in peace about the things tugging at her mind. Her family. Nicolas.

It was a relief not to be under the watchful eye of so many masters in the big house, and for once Suzette felt grateful to be surrounded by people who looked like her. Living in the big house had made her forget this other self. She had been ashamed by the way her mother talked, the coarse clothes her sisters wore. All the distance and embarrassment had been forgotten tonight, until she'd looked over Solataire's shoulder and caught herself in the mirror of Eugene Daurat's eyes.

She walked sure-footed through the thick mass of pine trees, all the way down to her thinking rock on the bank of Cane River, a place she had found a few years past, after Oreline grew into more confidence and stopped pulling at her every minute.

As Suzette looked off across the river, standing by her rock, she heard the soft squish of boots against mud, signaling a man's approach. Someone had followed her to her secret place.

'Ah, *ma chère*, I thought you would never stop walking,' Eugene Daurat said as he emerged from the woods, slightly out of breath.

'I'm going right back.' Suzette glanced nervously in the direction of the party, as if she could wish herself back to the center of the dance floor, surrounded by other people. 'I just came away from the party to cool off.'

'And are you so cool already?'

'It felt good to walk, M'sieu Eugene.'

'Better for the young than for those of us who are older, I'm afraid,' he said. 'That's a pretty dress. A little thin for this time of year, but you make it look just right. If you are cold, I could lend you my coat.'

'I think I should get back now, M'sieu.' Her voice sounded thin and tinny to her own ears.

'Just stay here with me for a little bit until I catch my breath. I might not be able to find my way back without you.'

The frightful pounding behind Suzette's small breasts would not slow its pace. She wanted to run but was afraid of insulting such a close friend of the master and mistress's. And he had said her dress was pretty.

'The music will guide you back.'

'Just give me a minute, Suzette.'

He sat on the rock, in no particular hurry.

'You seem different tonight than you do in the house,' Eugene said. 'Why is that?'

'Mam'zelle Oreline and I practiced the steps of the quadrille for the soirée last summer. I hadn't had a chance to dance them so much before.'

'I see. You dance them as well as any I've seen. Even in France.'

'Really?'

'*Oui*. When I saw you dance, you reminded me of my home in France. A town called Bordeaux. I miss it.'

Suzette was curious. 'Why would I remind you of France, M'sieu Eugene?'

'In France, they are full of life. You are full of life.' Eugene patted a spot next to him on the rock. 'Come, sit next to me for a moment.'

What was she supposed to say? What was she supposed to do? Was he making fun of her? Did the Derbannes know he was here with her, talking like this? Suzette edged closer toward the rock. 'It isn't right, M'sieu Eugene. I can just stand.'

'Nonsense,' Eugene said. 'You're cold. No more discussion. Come here.'

Suzette cautiously balanced herself on the far\flat edge of the rock, sitting but leaning away from the doll man.

Eugene moved close to Suzette and put his coat around her. 'I think you are so vibrant, Suzette. So full of joi de vivre. You make me forget myself.'

She was trembling and could think of nothing to say.

'The Derbannes say you are a good Catholic girl. Maybe you weren't thinking so much of the church when you were dancing tonight, eh? You have babies yet, little Suzette?'

'No, M'sieu.' Babies? Babies were for after she and Nicolas Mulon made plans.

The moon's rays shimmering on the water's surface broke in odd places, confusing her. She felt rooted to this spot, Eugene now sitting by her side on her special rock, his arm around her shoulder. It wasn't real, being talked to in such soft tones by a white man with a last name. He shifted his position and rested his hand on her knee, as if it were his right. Would it show poor upbringing to protest? To run? Suzette stared at Eugene Daurat's little feet, unwilling to bring her eyes up any farther than that. Casually he reached under her dress, under her bloomers, his hand cold and deliberate against her bare skin. She heard the sound of his jagged breathing and smelled the sharpness of liquor as it oozed from his pores.

'Lay back, Suzette.'

'I am a good girl, M'sieu.'

'Yes, I am sure you are.'

His voice didn't sound the same, as if it were coming from somewhere lower and deeper as he pressed her back onto the unforgiving rock. He moved above her, making strange noises in his throat while he undid the buttons of his britches with his free hand. He was heavy for a man so small. Everything was moving slowly, as if it had nothing at all to do with her. Like during a bad storm when the water rose on the river so fast that you could only watch it spill the banks, and nothing any man did could stop it. He moved back and forth, back and forth, pinning her, and she froze in the inescapable certainty of the moment. Nicolas, she thought unexpectedly. Nicolas should come and pull the doll man away, take her back to the party, ask her to dance; but try as she might she could conjure up only his name and not the kindness of Nicolas's face. Eugene's knee pried her open and he pushed into her, delivering pain to a central place. He stayed on top of her, dead weight grinding her hip and shoulder into the rock, catching his breath as if he had run a long race, forcing her to breathe in the flat smell of brandy and cigars that escaped from him as she could not.

'*Merci, ma chère*,' he said raggedly, but he still didn't move.

When at last he got up from her, careful not to get mud on himself, he looked away and busied himself straightening his clothes.

'You'd better go back now and join the party,' he said.

It was over. Suzette looked down, and even in the dull moonlight she could see that her beautiful white dress was streaked with traces of scarlet. She would need to wash it out in secret, she thought, make sure her mother never saw the stains. She needed to figure out how to change her dress and go back to the party before she was missed, what to do next. She wanted to ask the doll man his advice. The cold of the night pressed in as she waited for him to initiate some further connection, but he made no move toward her, had nothing else to say. Uncertain, with Eugene's back still to her, she forced herself up and started to walk in the direction of the music, listening for a sound, any sound, that would tell her the proper thing to do. There were party noises in the distance, festive sounds. She heard night calls from the woods, skittering creatures out prowling for food or trying to avoid becoming some bigger prey's next meal. There were river noises, gentle and soothing, as the edges of the water lapped at the red banks of the shore in a centuries-old ceremony of give-and-take.

But all that Suzette could make out was a sound just this side of hearing, like dreams drifting out of reach, slight as a soft spring wind.

HARRIET JACOBS

Extract from:

Incidents in the Life of a Slave Girl

Harriet Jacobs was born a slave in North Carolina in 1813. When she was six years old, her mother died and she grew up under the care of her mother's mistress, who taught her to read and write. After the death of this mistress, Harriet was given to her niece, but she was only a young child, whose father became Harriet's new master. He was cruel and unrelenting but after ten years Harriet managed to escape. She lived in a tiny space in her grand-mother's attic for seven years before fleeing to

Philadelphia and then New York, where she lived as a free woman. Her narrative was published in 1861. In this extract, Harriet Jacobs tells how even the choice of a boyfriend or husband is denied to a slave.

Why does the slave ever love? Why allow the tendrils of the heart to twine around objects which may at any moment be wrenched away by the hand of violence? When separations come by the hand of death, the pious soul can bow in resignation, and say, 'Not my will, but thine be done, O Lord!' But when the ruthless hand of a man strikes the blow, regardless of the misery he causes, it is hard to be submissive. I did not reason thus when I was a young girl. Youth will be youth. I loved and I indulged the hope that the dark clouds around me would turn out a bright lining; I forgot that in the land of my birth the shadows are too dense for light to penetrate. A land

Where laughter is not mirth; nor thought the mind;
Nor words a language; nor e'en men mankind.

Where cries reply to curses, shrieks to blows,
And each is tortured in his separate hell.

There was in the neighborhood a young colored carpenter; a free-born man. We had been well acquainted in childhood, and frequently met together afterwards. We became mutually attached, and he proposed to marry me. I loved him with all the ardor of a young girl's first love. But when I reflected that I was a slave, and that the laws gave no sanction to the marriage of such, my heart sank within me. My lover wanted to buy me; but I knew that Dr Flint was too wilful and arbitrary a man to consent to that arrangement. From him, I was sure of experiencing all sort of opposition, and I had nothing to hope from my mistress. She would have been delighted to have got rid of me, but not in that way. It would have relieved her mind of a burden if she could have seen me sold to some distant state, but if I was married near home I should be just as much in her husband's power as I had previously been, – for the husband of a slave has no power to protect her.

Moreover, my mistress, like many others, seemed to think that slaves had no right to any family ties of their own; that they were created merely to wait upon the family of the mistress. I once heard her abuse a young slave girl, who told her that a colored man wanted to make her his wife. 'I will have you peeled and pickled, my lady,' said she, 'if I ever hear you mention that subject again. Do you suppose that I will have you tending *my* children with the children of that nigger?' The girl to whom she said this had a mulatto child, of course not acknowledged by its father. The poor black man who loved her would have been proud to acknowledge his helpless offspring.

Many and anxious were the thoughts I revolved in my mind. I was at a loss what to do. Above all things, I was desirous to spare my lover the insults that had cut so deeply into my own soul. I talked with my grandmother about it, and partly told her my fears. I did not dare to tell her the worst. She had long suspected all was not right, and if I confirmed her suspicions I knew a storm would rise that would prove the overthrow of all my hopes.

This love-dream had been my support through many trials; and I could not bear to run the risk of having it suddenly dissipated. There was a lady in the neighborhood, a particular friend of Dr Flint's, who often visited the house. I had a great respect for her, and she had always manifested a friendly interest in me. Grandmother thought she would have great influence with the doctor. I went to this lady, and told her my story. I told her I was aware that my lover's being a free-born man would prove a great objection; but he wanted to buy me; and if Dr Flint would consent to that arrangement, I felt sure he would be willing to pay any reasonable price. She knew that Mrs Flint disliked me; therefore, I ventured to suggest that perhaps my mistress would approve of my being sold, as that would rid her of me. The lady listened with kindly sympathy, and promised to do her utmost to promote my wishes. She had an interview with the doctor, and I believe she pleaded my cause earnestly; but it was all to no purpose.

How I dreaded my master now! Every minute I expected to be summoned to his presence; but the day passed, and I heard nothing from him. The next morning, a message was brought to me: 'Master wants you in his study.' I found the door ajar, and I stood a moment gazing at the hateful man who claimed a right to rule me, body and soul. I entered, and tried to appear calm. I did not want him to know how my heart was bleeding. He looked fixedly at me, with an expression which seemed to say, 'I have half a mind to kill you on the spot.' At last he broke the silence, and that was a relief to both of us.

'So you want to be married, do you?' said he, 'and to a free nigger.'

'Yes, sir.'

'Well, I'll soon convince you whether I am your master, or the nigger fellow you honor so highly. If you *must* have a husband, you may take up with one of my slaves.'

What a situation I should be in, as the wife of one of *his* slaves, even if my heart had been interested.

I replied, 'Don't you suppose, sir, that a slave can

have some preference about marrying? Do you suppose that all men are alike to her?'

'Do you love this nigger?' said he, abruptly.

'Yes, sir.'

'How dare you tell me so!' he exclaimed, in great wrath. After a slight pause, he added, 'I supposed you thought more of yourself; that you felt above the insults of such puppies.'

I replied, 'If he is a puppy I am a puppy, for we are both of the negro race. It is right and honorable for us to love each other. The man you call a puppy never insulted me, sir; and he would not love me if he did not believe me to be a virtuous woman.'

He sprang upon me like a tiger, and gave me a stunning blow. It was the first time he had ever struck me; and fear did not enable me to control my anger. When I had recovered a little from the effects, I exclaimed, 'You have struck me for answering you honestly! How I despise you!'

There was silence for some minutes. Perhaps he was deciding what should be my punishment; or, perhaps, he wanted to give me time to reflect on what

I had said, and to whom I had said it. Finally, he asked, 'Do you know what you have said?'

'Yes, sir; but your treatment drove me to it.'

'Do you know that I have a right to do as I like with you, – that I can kill you, if I please?'

'You have tried to kill me, and I wish you had; but you have no right to do as you like with me.'

'Silence!' he exclaimed, in a thundering voice. 'By heavens, girl, you forget yourself too far! Are you mad? If you are, I will soon bring you to your senses. Do you think any other master would bear what I have borne from you this morning? Many masters would have killed you on the spot. How would you like to be sent to jail for your insolence?'

'I know I have been disrespectful, sir,' I replied; 'but you drove me to it; I couldn't help it. As for the jail, there would be more peace for me there than there is here.'

'You deserve to go there,' said he, 'and to be under such treatment, that you would forget the meaning of the word *peace*. It would do you good. It would take some of your high notions out of you. But I am not ready to send you there yet, notwithstanding your ingratitude for all my kindness and forbearance. You have been the plague of my life. I have wanted to make you happy, and I have been repaid with the basest ingratitude; but though you have proved yourself incapable of appreciating my kindness, I will be lenient towards you, Linda. I will give you one more chance to redeem your character. If you behave yourself and do as I require, I will forgive you and treat you as I always have done; but if you disobey me, I will punish you as I would the meanest slave on my plantation. Never let me hear that fellow's name mentioned again. If I ever know of your speaking to him, I will cowhide you both; and if I catch him lurking about my premises, I will shoot him as soon as I would a dog. Do you hear what I say? I'll teach you a lesson about marriage and free niggers! Now go, and let this be the last time I have occasion to speak to you on this subject.'

Reader, did you ever hate? I hope not. I never did but once; and I trust I never shall again. Somebody has called it 'the atmosphere of hell'; and I believe it is so.

For a fortnight the doctor did not speak to me. He thought to mortify me; to make me feel that I had disgraced myself by receiving the honorable address-es of a respectable colored man, in preference to the base proposals of a white man. But though his lips disdained to address me, his eyes were very loquacious. No animal has ever watched its prey more narrowly than he watched me. He knew that I could write, though he had failed to make me read his letters; and he was now troubled lest I should exchange letters with another man. After a while he became weary of silence; and I was sorry for it. One morning, as he passed through the hall, to leave the house, he contrived to thrust a note into my hand. I thought I had better read it, and spare myself the vexation of having him read it to me. It expressed regret for the blow he had given me, and reminded me that I myself was wholly to blame for it. He hoped I had become convinced of the injury I was doing myself by incurring his displeasure. He wrote that he had made up his mind to go to Louisiana; that he should take several slaves with him, and intended I should be one of the number. My mistress would remain where she was; therefore I should have nothing to fear from that quarter. If I merited kindness from him, he assured me that it would be lavishly bestowed. He begged me to think over the matter, and answer the following day.

The next morning I was called to carry a pair of scissors to his room. I laid them on the table, with the letter beside them. He thought it was my answer, and did not call me back. I went as usual to attend my young mistress to and from school. He met me in the street, and ordered me to stop at his office on my way back. When I entered, he showed me his letter, and asked me why I had not answered it. I replied, 'I am your daughter's property, and it is in your power to send me, or take me, wherever you please.' He said he was very glad to find me so willing to go, and that we should start early in the autumn. He had a large practice in the town, and I rather thought he had made up the story merely to frighten me. However that might be, I was determined that I would never go to Louisiana with him.

Summer passed away, and early in the autumn Dr Flint's eldest son was sent to Louisiana to examine the country, with a view to emigrating. That news did not disturb me. I knew very well that I should not be sent with him. That I had not been taken to the plantation before this time, was owing to the fact that his son was there. He was jealous of his son; and jealousy of the overseer had kept him from punishing me by sending me into the fields to work. Is it strange that I was not proud of these protectors? As for the overseer, he was a man for whom I had less respect than I had for a bloodhound.

Young Mr Flint did not bring back a favorable report of Louisiana, and I heard no more of that scheme. Soon after this, my lover met me at the corner of the street, and I stopped to speak to him. Looking up, I saw my master watching us from his window. I hurried home, trembling with fear. I was sent for, immediately, to go to his room. He met me with a blow. 'When is mistress to be married?'

said he, in a sneering tone. A shower of oaths and imprecations followed. How thankful I was that my lover was a free man! That my tyrant had no power to flog him for speaking to me in the street!

Again and again I revolved in my mind how all this would end. There was no hope that the doctor would consent to sell me on any terms. He had an iron will, and was determined to keep me, and to conquer me. My lover was an intelligent and religious man. Even if he could have obtained permission to marry me while I was a slave, the marriage would give him no power to protect me from my master. It would have made him miserable to witness the insults I should have been subjected to. And then, if we had children, I knew they must 'follow the condition of the mother'. What a terrible blight that would be on the heart of a free, intelligent father! For *his* sake, I felt that I ought not to link his fate with my own unhappy destiny. He was going to Savannah to see about a little property left him by an uncle; and hard as it was to bring my feelings to it, I earnestly entreated him not to come back. I advised him to go to the Free States, where his tongue would not be tied, and where his intelligence would be of more avail to him. He left me, still hoping the day would come when I could be bought. With me the lamp of hope had gone out. The dream of my girlhood was over. I felt lonely and desolate.

PART THREE

SLAVERY IN BRITAIN

SANDRA AGARD

Runaway

The boy's heart felt heavy and pain racked his whole body. He coughed and began to choke. He gulped greedily for the cold night air; but that made him cough even more and he was promptly sick, bringing up the supper of potatoes he had eaten earlier that day.

He needed to rest but he was afraid to stop even for the shortest time. He had to keep running; as far as he could in a land that was strange to him. He had never been in the countryside on his own before and the tall trees, hanging vines and hidden ditches frightened him. He would never have gone alone into the woods surrounding his home back in Jamaica – full, he was sure, of demons like jumbies and duppies. He was not sure what the demons were in this strange land, but he felt they were there . . . watching him, ready to tear him apart.

It was so still in these woods. It seemed that the steady rain had scared off all the creatures of the night. Even the air was different here. Back home it had been so hot, but with cooling rain. Here it was freezing cold and it went deep into your bones. He was glad he had taken the heavy coat belonging to Thomas, the stable boy. He allowed himself a slight smile as he thought of him finding his favourite coat missing. Thomas had made his life such a misery since he had arrived in the English countryside. He had laughed at him, pinched and punched him whenever he could. Now the boy's prize was weighing heavily on him; but he dare not leave it – they would know which way he had come, for he had no time to bury it deeply in the earth.

How he missed Jamaica, his homeland, and his friends Kwesi and Kwaku, and Mama Rae with all her stories. It had been so hard to say goodbye. He had tried not to remember: it hurt too much. He knew he should only be thinking of getting away from the Big House as fast as he could before they discovered that he was missing.

He thanked the Lord that it was a moonless night and the clouds hung low and heavy with rain. That should put them off his tracks for a while, he thought. It was slippery and muddy and it was hard to follow the paths, but he had a head start – everybody would be busy with the grand ball. He should have been by his mistress's side, keeping her cool and fresh with his peacock fan. But now there was someone else in his place. Since leaving London six months ago he had noticed a change in his mistress's manner towards him. She often snapped at him and dismissed him abruptly from her chambers. Only the night before, she had told him angrily to get out of her sight; his face turned hot with the memory. He had tried so hard to please her, but once again he had failed. He could not under-stand what he had done. The mistress had always been so kind to him. Not like the master, with his dark and angry moods; his heavy boots often did his talking for him. The boy had always tried hard to avoid his lordship's presence.

Unfortunately, Thomas had heard about this latest fall from grace and had sneered gleefully as he ate his evening meal in the kitchen.

'Now even the mistress can see you for what you are – a little devil,' he had said. 'Soon you'll be mine, boy! Nobody will care what happens to you. Nobody!' And he had laughed. Even the other servants and Cook had joined in the laughter.

It was then that the idea of running away came to him. But he had not realized then how soon he would be putting his plan into action.

His right knee ached from his wild scramble to get away, but he could not stop to tend to it. He had to keep running before they closed in on him. So ignoring the sharp jabs of pain, he stumbled on through the thorns and brambles that tore at his bruised and bleeding skin. He prayed that this road would carry him swiftly to London. He had spent his first year there, until her ladyship decided to live in the countryside. He knew he could lose himself in the winding streets and this he must do quickly – hopefully amongst the Blackbirds of St Paul's; the poor coloured men and boys who slept around the great cathedral. After all, George, one of his lordship's hound-handlers, had run away to the busy city nearly a year ago. His lordship had not been able to find him despite posting runaway notices around the countryside and offering generous rewards.

The thought of running away scared him; he remembered those who had escaped from the plantation. Many had been caught and were punished severely, losing a hand or a foot. He must not be caught.

The boy had no idea how far London was. But he knew he was on the right road, for he had often accompanied his ladyship in the carriage to the Coach Station Inn, and that was on the London Road. The inn was always full of people – merchants and their servants, sailors, labourers; all talking about the rich streets of London.

How different it had been only a month before,

when he had been her ladyship's firm favourite, at her side constantly. But gradually his presence had begun to anger her: she accused him of being too big, too clumsy. He had noticed the changes in his body as he continued to grow and grow, needing yet another blue velvet suit. His lordship had not been pleased by the extra cost and had let the boy know his displeasure with a heavy kick to his leg.

Now he felt the stinging tears of hurt and disappointment he had been fighting for so long. He felt so alone and afraid. He knew he should go on, but he was tired and in pain. It would not hurt to stop for a little while to regain his strength. So he simply curled up in a ditch and gave himself up to the memories of the bright lights of Regency Hall and the grand ball that had led to his flight on this moonless night.

'No, Mary. Not the sapphires. The pearls. They are more fitting for this dress,' said Lady Derby. 'Bring the pearls!'

Mary, Lady Derby's maid, hurried over to the chest

and, in her haste, knocked over a pink rose-decorated porcelain bowl of white powder.

'Mary, do be careful. That's the finest Chinese face powder!' cried Lady Derby.

'Sorry, ma'am,' whispered Mary, trying to make amends by brushing the powder back into the bowl.

'Leave it. You're only making it worse. Just bring the pearls – and why is that window not open? It's far too hot in here!' she added crossly.

'You told me to close it, ma'am – you didn't want the night air to harm your delicate skin before the ball,' said Mary, placing the pearls before Lady Derby and then hurrying to open the window.

'Yes, yes,' sighed Lady Derby with a dismissive wave of her hand. 'Where is that boy? Scipio . . . Scipio?' she called.

A door opened and a small black boy aged around seven entered the room.

He was dressed in a dark-blue velvet page suit. On his head he wore a white silk turban; in his right ear, a large hooped silver earring. He held a huge peacock fan. It seemed to overwhelm him, but he carried it with confidence. One almost did not see the silver collar that hung tightly around his neck. He approached Lady Derby, bowed, then stood to attention like a soldier in His Majesty's army and waited.

'Scipio, I should not have to call you. Your place is by my side,' said Lady Derby, eyeing the small boy sharply.

'I . . . I'm sorry, your ladyship, but last night you . . . you told me to go away and I was unsure whether to return . . .' he mumbled softly.

'Yes, yes. Your work is becoming very careless. You seem be growing lazier day by day. I might have to look for a replacement. You would not like that, would you, Scipio?'

'No . . . no, your ladyship,' said Scipio hastily. 'I'll try much harder.' Biting his lips to hold back tears, he began to fan Lady Derby.

'Much better.' She closed her eyes and leaned back in her chair.

The door opened again and a large, red-haired, middle-aged man came rushing in carrying a newspaper. He looked angrily at Scipio.

'That boy should not be in your inner chambers. How often have I told you?' he cried. His voice was deep and harsh. The boy tried to hide behind the fan.

'He is getting too big for his own good. We are obviously feeding him too well! He should not be in a lady's chambers.' The man continued shouting, slamming the newspaper on the table and causing more of the precious powder to fall on the floor.

'Oh, Charles, I wish you would not keep fussing so much. The boy is quite harmless. He has been in my service since Captain McKenzie brought him off the ship as a pup. He's obedient, well mannered and softly spoken; if a little careless at times—' began Lady Derby.

'And will likely cut our throats as we sleep at night as they're doing in West Indies now.' Lord Derby hit the newspaper sharply. 'Growing too quickly for my liking. He should be in the fields, not in the house!' he concluded stubbornly.

'What has upset you, my dear?' asked Lady Derby. 'Mary, fetch his lordship some water.' She waved a finger at Scipio, who stopped fanning her and stepped back awkwardly. He did not dare go near the door, for Lord Derby's broad frame was blocking his escape. He did not wish to feel his boot again; he had already endured the taunts of Thomas that morning.

Mary hurried across the room to the water pitcher. She filled a glass, brought it over to Lord Derby and gave it to him with a curtsey. He grabbed it, spilling some of its contents onto one of the Persian rugs that lay on the floor. He finished the rest in one loud gulp.

'What is wrong, Charles? You've been in such a terrible temper all week. I hope you'll feel better before the guests arrive. You're not even dressed yet. They will be arriving soon. Mary, do my hair now.' Lady Derby picked up a jade-encrusted hand mirror and admired her reflection.

Lord Derby stared at his wife, a look of fury on his face. 'This blasted ball. It's costing me a fortune. Is it really necessary?'

It was his wife's turn to look furious. 'Well, it's too late to cancel it now. Everything is ready – except you! Of course it is necessary. We've been over this countless times. How are we going to meet the best families if we do not court them first. We've been away too long in the West Indies; so much has changed in England. How does one wear one's hair these days? What is the right cut of one's dress? And look at my face. The women all have such pale complexions here. I'm almost as dark as Mary and Scipio. That awful sun in Jamaica has simply ruined my skin! And you ask me if this ball is really necessary. It certainly is! We need to be English again. This is where we belong. Here in the country we can make our mark. It was time to come back!'

She picked up the mirror again and Mary gently brushed hair that was already in place.

Lord Derby sighed. 'The news from Jamaica is bad. More slaves are rebelling. It's only a matter of time before the worst happens. The plantations will fail and where will we be then?'

'We'll be here. Home and safe,' she said. 'Now please get dressed. The first guests will be here soon. Mary, bring my ivory shawl.'

Mary went quickly over to a large redwood

wardrobe. She glanced at Scipio, who was standing against the wall, and smiled the briefest of smiles. He returned the smile – a smile that unfortunately Lord Derby caught.

He leaped up and grabbed Scipio roughly by the shoulder. 'What're you planning?' he yelled, his round face red with anger.

'Nothing . . . nothing, my lord,' stammered Scipio. His heart was racing.

'Going to murder us in our beds just like your friends back in Jamaica!' Lord Derby continued to shake him, his grey eyes glaring down at the small boy.

Scipio did not know what to say and gripped the peacock fan. He could feel tears welling up inside him; he fought desperately to keep them away. The master hated weakness and he would get a beating if he showed any.

Scipio could see Mary trembling by the wardrobe, her eyes averted. Even Lady Derby looked away: she knew that when her husband was in this mood, there was no stopping him.

Scipio realized there would be no help from anyone in the room, so he braced himself for the blows that would surely come. However, a sharp knock at the door saved him.

'Come in!' cried Lady Derby in a high-pitched voice.

John, one of the servants, entered and bowed. 'My lord, Captain McKenzie has arrived and awaits your presence in the library.' He bowed again and then stood upright, awaiting instructions.

'What does he want? He wasn't invited to the ball,' said Lady Derby. 'He's so crude. Charles, please conclude your business before our guests arrive.'

'That "business" keeps you in the best finery. It would be good for you to remember that, my dear! Captain McKenzie's fleet of ships are still doing fine trade despite this growing trouble in the West Indies. Besides, he has brought you a gift – something I'm sure you'll approve of,' said Lord Derby, and with these last words he eyed Scipio with a sly smile on his lips.

Scipio shuddered and tried to disappear further

within the soft feathers of the peacock fan. For some reason he felt worse than ever. There had been something so menacing in his lordship's smile.

Lady Derby failed to notice the discomfort of her young pageboy; instead she eagerly turned to her husband and said: 'A gift? I wonder what it could be. Some fine Indian rugs, precious jewels' – her eyes glowed greedily – 'or some Chinese silk . . . a new servant? If so, then I must have my portrait done. I hear that portrait painting is now the height of fashion in London,' she added excitedly. 'Mary – my shawl. Scipio, go to the ballroom. Mary, do hurry up!'

Scipio stepped out of Lord Derby's reach and ran from the room as fast as he could. He wished for the hundredth time that he would stop growing; then maybe life would get back to how it was before he was put on board the big ship that had carried him so far away from his Jamaican homeland. The mistress had liked him back then; why had it gone so wrong?

Scipio had been so lost in thought, he almost bumped into Thomas, who grabbed the fan, seized

Scipio by the arm and pushed him roughly into an alcove in the hallway. Scipio tried to get away but Thomas was too strong and held him tightly, his strong fingers bruising him.

'Let me go! Let me go!' cried Scipio.

Thomas simply laughed at Scipio's useless struggles. 'Not the favourite any more, are you?' he sneered. 'His lordship never really liked you. Not the favourite with her ladyship for much longer either. Thinking you're better than us with your fancy clothes and fine words. Why, you're no better than his lordship's swine!' Thomas then twisted Scipio's arm and shoved him to the floor, tossed the peacock fan in his face and spat at him.

'By the way, you might as well say goodbye to that pretty fan, for Captain McKenzie's gift to his ladyship will now use it. He's one of your kind. They call him Pompey. Does not speak, they say. Small and as dark as the night; another of the Devil's children. No matter, I'll soon whip him into shape. Just like I'll soon whip you!' Laughing, he left the dazed and puzzled Scipio alone on the floor.

What had Thomas meant? Another like him? A new pageboy for his mistress? Then what would happen to him? Had he finally outgrown his stay in the Big House?

Scipio knew then that he had no other choice but to run away. Something was going on that involved him, for Captain McKenzie meant trouble. It was on one of the captain's ships that Scipio had come to England. The captain had hated the small boy: he could have sold him elsewhere for a lot more money. But his lordship had promised his wife a gift . . .

Yes, he would run in a day or two. He had to plan his escape carefully. He got up, dusted down his clothes, straightened the peacock fan and quietly slipped into the ballroom. He stood near one of the large windows and watched the carriages arrive, their runners lighting the way in the approaching twilight. He too had been looking forward to the ball – maybe one of the other pages would have news of his plantation back in Jamaica; but now not even that could cheer him up.

Scipio's thoughts were interrupted by a hand on his

shoulder. Startled, he turned round and saw Mary's concerned face looking at him.

'What—?' he began.

'Shh . . . not here!' she whispered quickly. 'Meet me in the old stables when you're dismissed.'

Scipio suddenly felt very cold. What was Mary talking about? 'But my mistress will need me,' he protested.

'Times are changing, and if you value your life you'll be there,' she hissed, and without another word she turned and left.

Scipio had no time to think further, for the doors opened, music began to play, and Lord and Lady Derby walked into the room followed by their guests.

Scipio hurried to where his master and mistress would sit and began to fan them both as they took their seats. In his haste he had not seen the last person to come in behind the guests. Indeed, all he could think of was pleasing his mistress and gaining her favour once again. He really did not want to leave her. London was so far away.

A month ago his mistress had usually nodded her head at him in approval; now she ignored him. Was he fanning her too fast or too slowly? he wondered. He did not know what to do.

'Enough, Scipio!' she snapped. 'Go to the kitchens! Pompey, take the fan!'

Scipio hesitated and stopped. Had he heard right? Pompey? Was this the new boy Thomas had mocked him with? The new boy who would take his place at his mistress's side. He tried once more to win back her favour.

'I'm sorry, mistress,' he said in a small voice. 'I . . . I only wish to serve you and—'

'Your service is no longer required here,' said Lady Derby, and she turned away to smile warmly at her guests.

'Your mistress gave you a command. Now do as she says before I take my boot to your pitiful dark skin. Go to the kitchens now! You'll be dealt with later,' said Lord Derby between clenched teeth. 'Pompey, the fan! Take it and do your duty now!'

To Scipio's horror a small black boy dressed in the

same dark-blue velvet page suit and white silk turban with a hooped silver earring appeared before Scipio and held out his brown hand for the fan. The heavy silver collar around his neck glinted against his dark complexion. He looked no older than five years old.

The new pageboy took the fan and eased into Scipio's place beside Lady Derby. His eyes were filled with pity for the dismissed Scipio, who stood lonely and sad amid the laughter and conversation of the ballroom.

Mary had known this would happen. How? He had to get to the stables to find out what was going on.

Head bowed, Scipio walked away from the ballroom, with its candlelight, laughter and music, and headed not for the kitchens but to the stables to hear his fate.

Mary was not there yet. Nobody was – not even the horses – for they had been moved the day before to another stable on the other side of the estate. Only the blacksmith's tools remained. Tools? It was then that he finally made up his mind to run. His mistress had always cared for him, or so he had thought. But something had changed, and for the first time since leaving Jamaica he was truly afraid. Yes, he must run. The silver collar would have to go. He picked up an iron file and tried to unpick the lock.

'Going somewhere, boy?' a voice hissed behind him.

He dropped the file, spun round and came face to face with Thomas.

'John sent me to find you. Got lost on your way to the kitchens? I followed you – wanted to know what you were up to. Never trusted your kind! You're the Devil's child! That's what Father Grey says every Sunday in church, and he's right!' Thomas spat at Scipio's feet and took a menacing step towards him.

Scipio did not reply. His eyes searched for a means of escape; but there was none.

'Trying to run away, boy? You won't get far. Besides, master's got plans for you. Where are your airs and graces now? Coming over here and lording it over us. Well, I'm going to teach you a lesson . . .'

He picked up a hammer and took another step towards Scipio.

Scipio picked up the iron file, ready to defend himself.

Thomas laughed. 'I'm going to enjoy this—' However, he was halted in mid sentence by a wooden bucket crashing down on his head. Both he and the hammer collapsed onto the stone floor.

'Always wanted to do that.' It was Mary with a look of triumph on her face.

Scipio slumped to the floor.

'No time to rest. You've to go!' She took the iron file from him and pushed it into the collar's lock. After a few minutes there was a sharp click and the collar clattered to the floor.

Scipio clutched his throat. It burned and felt sore. He began to rub it.

'Gently.' Mary looked at his neck. 'It'll hurt for a while; but it'll heal. Put this on it.' She gave him a piece of cloth. It was one of her ladyship's cotton handkerchiefs; it was slightly damp.

'I can't take this,' he protested.

'Don't worry. She has many. She'll not miss one – trust me. Get out of those clothes.' She handed him a pair of grey breeches and a loose brown sackcloth.

Scipio fumbled his way out of his blue velvet suit. The new clothes smelled of horses and scratched his skin.

'Hurry,' said Mary. 'Take this too,' and she handed him a small bundle. 'Food for the journey. It's all I could get. One more thing.' She bent over the unconscious Thomas, removed his overcoat and gave that to Scipio as well. He took it reluctantly; it smelled of Thomas.

'It's a little big, but it'll keep out the cold,' she said.

'But Mary, where shall I go?' he asked in a small voice.

'Take the London Road. You'll be safe in the city.'

Suddenly the idea of running away did not seem like a good one.

'Maybe I can talk to my mistress—' he began.

'Don't be a fool. You're now the property of

Captain McKenzie. You've been sold! His ship sets sail for the islands at first light—'

'Then I will go home—' said Scipio eagerly.

'You'll be put to work in the cane fields. Remember how harshly field slaves are treated on the plantations? You will be shown no mercy and will be worked to death,' said Mary. 'No, the only thing for you to do is run. Now, enough talking – go! The west gate is open: follow the path – that will lead you to the London Road. Only travel by night – daylight is too dangerous.'

But still Scipio did not move. 'My mistress would never agree to this,' he said stubbornly.

'She was there when the deal was made with Captain McKenzie. She doesn't care about you. She already has a new fan bearer. You saw him. They call him Pompey. He will not last long either. We all grow up sooner or later. Now you're wasting time and I must get back before I am missed.'

Scipio knew she was right. Deep down he knew he had lost the love of his mistress. Did he ever have it? he wondered.

'But what about you, Mary? What will happen to you?' he asked.

'I'll be fine. Someone has to stay behind to help. You might find George in London.'

'You helped George run?' said Scipio.

'Yes,' she replied.

'You're not afraid? If you're caught . . .' Scipio clutched the bundle to his chest.

'I'll be hung, drawn and quartered or sold. But until that day comes I'll be here to help those who run. Now go. God speed.'

Scipio walked towards the door, then stopped. 'Will I ever see you again?' he asked.

'Probably not,' she replied sadly.

He hesitated, trying to find the right words. At last he said: 'Thank you.'

'Be free — and Scipio, change your name. Now run!' she said, smiling warmly.

Without another word he fled into the moonless night, the sounds of the grand ball echoing behind him.

* * *

Scipio woke up from his dreams and for a moment wondered where he was. Instantly he remembered. He tried to sit up but his body hurt. He rubbed his knee and his arm where Thomas had bruised it earlier that day.

He looked up at the sky. The moon was still absent and the rain continued to fall steadily. He knew he must be on his way. So he picked up his bundle and wrapped the coat more tightly around his body.

He prayed Mary would be safe. The last thing she had told him was to change his name.

He thought of the stories Mama Rae had told him and recalled the tale of Cudjoe, who had led a slave rebellion in Jamaica.

Something moved amongst the bushes. He held his breath as a rabbit scampered across his path. It stopped for a brief moment to look at him and then was gone.

Suddenly he no longer felt afraid of the night's terrors; he knew what he must do. Ignoring his aching body, he stood up. The rain fell cold and refreshing onto his face; he welcomed it, for he was free.

He raised his arms as if he were with his friends Kwesi and Kwaku, talking at one of Mama Rae's secret meetings in the woods back in Jamaica.

'My friends, listen to me: from this night on I'm no longer Scipio. I'm Cudjoe – a free man!' And with renewed energy and hope he turned and ran into the night towards London.

BLACK PAGEBOYS

It became the fashion for wealthy people to buy young African boys and girls as pages and maids, sometimes giving them to their children. Many were sold in the thriving coffee houses of London, Bristol and Liverpool.

Some were given classical names like Scipio and Pompey. They were made to wear silver or brass collars and treated like pets. The darker the child the better, as this contrasted with the white skin of the owner.

Many of the boys quickly fell out of favour as they reached puberty. They were either sold on or ran away.

THE BLACKBIRDS OF ST PAUL'S CATHEDRAL

These were poor and destitute young black men and boys who had run away from their owners. They slept rough on the steps of St Paul's Cathedral.

SLAVE REVOLTS

There were numerous slaves revolts in the Caribbean

islands throughout the 1700s and 1800s. Resistance took many forms, from burning the master's dinner to burning down his plantation. Many of the owners did not live on their plantations, but ran their affairs from England. They were known as absentee landlords. One of the most notable slave revolts occurred in Saint Domingue in 1789: when news of the French Revolution reached the enslaved population, they demanded freedom like the revolutionaries. Forty thousand slaves led by Toussaint L'Ouverture revolted against the French, and the independent country of Haiti was declared soon after.

OLAUDAH EQUIANO

Extract from:

The Interesting Narrative of the Life of Olaudah Equiano

Olaudah Equiano was born in 1745 in what is now southeastern Nigeria. He was kidnapped and sold into slavery at the age of eleven. Transported to the West Indies, he was sold to an officer in the British Navy and served on board during the war against the French. He finally bought his own freedom in 1766. His autobiography was published in 1789 – at a time when slaves were still routinely traded into Britain – and was an inspiration to many other ex-slaves to write of their lives. The book is still in print over 200 years later.

The extract chosen shows how Equiano was to be horribly betrayed by the British officer who had promised him his freedom when the ship docked in England.

After our ship was fitted out again for service, in September she went to Guernsey, where I was very glad to see my old hostess, who was now a widow, and my former little charming companion her daughter. I spent some time here very happily with them, till October, when we had orders to repair to Portsmouth. We parted from each other with a great deal of affection, and I promised to return soon, and see them again, not knowing what all-powerful fate had determined for me. Our ship having arrived at Portsmouth, we went into the harbour, and remained there till the end of November, when we heard great talk about peace; and, to our very great joy, in the beginning of December we had orders to go up to London with our ship, to be paid off. We received this news with loud huzzas, and every other demonstration of gladness; and nothing but mirth was to be seen through every part of the ship. I too was not without my share of the general joy on this occasion. I thought now of nothing but being freed, and working for myself, and thereby getting money to enable me to get a good education; for I always had a great desire to be able at least to read and write; and while I was on shipboard I had endeavoured to improve myself in both. While I was in the Aetna particularly, the captain's clerk taught me to write, and gave me a smattering of arithmetic as far as the rule of three. There was also one Daniel Queen, about forty years of age, a man very well educated, who messed with me on board this ship, and he likewise dressed and attended the captain. Fortunately this man soon became very much attached to me, and took very great pains to instruct me in many things. He taught me to shave and dress hair a little, and also to read in the Bible, explaining many passages to me, which I did not comprehend. I was wonderfully surprised to see the laws and rules of my country written almost exactly here; a circumstance which I believe tended to impress our manners and customs more deeply on my memory. I used to tell him of this resemblance; and many a time we had sat up the whole night together at this employment. In short he was like a father to me; and some even used to call me after his name; they also styled me the black Christian. Indeed I almost loved him with the affection of a son. Many things I have denied myself that he might have them; and when I used to play at marbles, or any other game, and won a few halfpence, or got any little money, which I did sometimes, for shaving any one, I used to buy him a little sugar or tobacco, as far as my stock of money would go. He used to say, that he and I never should part; and that when our ship was paid off, as I was as free as himself or any other man on board, he would instruct me in his business, by which I might gain a good livelihood. This gave me new life and spirits, and my heart burned within me, while I thought the time long till I obtained my freedom: for though my master had not promised it to me, yet besides the assurances I had received that he had no right to detain me, he always treated me with the greatest kindness, and reposed in me an unbounded confidence; he even paid attention to my morals; and would never suffer me to deceive him, or tell lies, of which he used to tell me the consequences; and that if I did so, God would not love me; so that from all this tenderness, I had never once supposed, in all my dreams of freedom, that he would think of detaining me any longer than I wished.

In pursuance of our orders we sailed from Portsmouth for the Thames, and arrived at Deptford the 10th of December; where we cast anchor just as it was high water. The ship was up about half an hour, when my master ordered the barge to be manned; and all in an instant, without having before given me the least reason to suspect any thing of the matter, he forced me into the barge, saying, I was going to leave him, but he would take care I should not. I was so struck with the unexpectedness of this proceeding, that for some time I could not make a reply, only I made an offer to go for my books and chest of clothes, but he swore I should not move out of his sight; and if I did he would cut my throat, at the same time taking his hanger. I began, however, to collect myself: and, plucking up courage, I told him I was free, and he could not by law serve me so. But this only enraged him the more; and he continued to swear, and said he would soon let me know whether he would or not, and at that instant sprung himself into the barge from the ship, to the astonishment and sorrow of all on board. The tide, rather unluckily for me, had just turned downward, so that we quickly fell down the river along with it, till we came among some outward-bound West-Indiamen; for he was resolved to put me on board the first vessel he could get to receive me. The boat's crew, who pulled against their will, became quite faint at different times, and would have gone ashore; but he would not let them. Some of them strove then to cheer me, and told me he could not sell me, and that they would stand by me, which revived me a little, and encouraged my hopes; for as they pulled along he asked some vessels to receive me, and they would not. But, just as we had got a little below Gravesend, we came alongside of a ship which was going away the next tide for the West Indies; her name was the Charming Sally, Capt. James Doran; and my master went on board and agreed with him for me; and in a little time I was sent for into the cabin. When I came there, Captain Doran asked me if I knew him. I answered that I did not; 'Then,' said he 'you are now my slave.' I told him my master could not sell me to him, nor to any one else. 'Why,' said he, 'did not your master buy you?' I confessed he did. But I have served him, said I, many years, and he has taken all my wages and prize-money, for I only got one sixpence during the war; besides this I have been baptized; and by the laws of the land no man has a right to sell me; and I added, that I had heard a lawyer, and others at different times, tell my master so. They both then said that those people who told me so were not my friends: but I replied – It was very extraordinary that other people did not know the law as well as they. Upon this Captain Doran said I talked too much English;

and if I did not behave myself well, and be quiet, he had a method on board to make me. I was too well convinced of his power over me to doubt what he said: and my former sufferings in the slave-ship presenting themselves to my mind, the recollection of them made me shudder. However, before I retired, I told them that as I could not get any right among men here, I hoped I should hereafter in Heaven; and I immediately left the cabin, filled with resentment and sorrow. The only coat I had with me my master took away with him, and said, 'If your prize-money had been 10,000£ I had a right to it all, and would have taken it.' I had about nine guineas, which during my long sea-faring life, I had scraped together from trifling perquisites and little ventures; and I hid it that instant, lest my master should take that from me likewise, still hoping that by some means or other I should make my escape to the shore, and indeed some of my old shipmates told me not to despair, for they would get me back again; and that, as soon as they could get their pay, they would immediately come to Portsmouth to me, where this ship was going: but, alas! all my hopes were baffled, and the hour of my deliverance was yet far off. My master, having soon concluded his bargain with the captain, came out of the cabin, and he and his people got into the boat, and put off; I followed them with aching eyes as long as I could, and when they were out of sight I threw myself on the deck, with a heart ready to burst with sorrow and anguish.

CATHERINE JOHNSON

The Last Words of Cato Hopkins, a Negro, being thirteen years of age or thereabouts

Newgate Prison, London
October 15th, the year of Our Lord, 1710

'How'd I come into the profession?'

The Newgate ordinary sat in front of me on a stool he'd brought with him.

'I know your game!' I said. 'You'll have this all down and sold to some penny ballad seller before my body's cold!' I looked away and would have walked away too, but the chains bit into my wrists and ankles. 'You'll call it "The Boy Who Made the *Favourite* Disappear!" Or "The Ship That Vanished" or some such nonsense!'

'It's a long night,' the ordinary said, 'the one before you hang. No one's called for you, there'll be no one in the mob to cut you down and save you from the surgeons! They'll hand you over and take their shilling piece. Think on that, lad. And we'd all like to know what happened to the vessel in question. A three-master, it was.' He coughed. I looked the other way in case he could read my face, even here in the dark. 'And the gold she had on board of course. I mean, if there *was* anything you could tell me—'

'I am no snitch! I'll tell you nothing!'

The ordinary smiled. I shut my eyes. The dark of the condemned cell seemed just as dark whether you had your eyes open or closed. And to tell the truth, I felt more foolish that I was the only one of my 'family' to be caught for it. Indeed, to be caught for anything at all was bad enough . . . but to hang . . . that had to be nothing but my own stupidity.

The *Favourite's* vanishing was to be Mother Hopkins's final act, her last hurrah before old age slowed her, and I had let her down – no wonder no one asked for me.

I supposed my 'family', who were the nearest thing to blood relatives I could name, had vanished into the stew of the city. They must have reckoned me already good as dead. Mother Hopkins – the woman who'd been as near a mother as any – never showed her face at my trial. I called her Mother; she taught me everything I know, reading, writing, the way to spring any lock you like, but she never bore me in the natural way. Paid threepence for me, she says, not that you can believe a word from her lips – I don't know why I should even care a fig for any of them.

But there's a lump in my throat feels like it's the size of a cannonball.

'*The* Mother Hopkins?' the ordinary asked. I nodded and his face lit up. 'I remember the woman myself! In here to swing like you, she was. Not thirteen, fourteen years ago!' He rubbed his chin as if that action eased his memory. 'A fine-looking woman.'

I said nothing. Mother Hopkins, although possessed of many qualities, such as cunning, cleverness and the ability to part a gentleman from his money without said gentleman realizing, would not, in my mind, be thought of as fine looking.

The ordinary sighed. 'Knew her well,' he said. 'Once.'

This was not a surprise. Mother Hopkins knew most of the useful people in London. I had heard the tale of how she escaped the condemned cell, and my infant part in that story (she would never have paid anything for me if I wasn't to be useful). But it seemed as if her cunning and cleverness would no longer be used to further my own little life.

None of the others had showed themselves. Not Bella, although to be honest I never expected to see her anyway. Sam Caesar and Jack Goodwin were nowhere to be seen. Addeline came once, on the day the beak passed sentence. He wore his black cap as he brought down the hammer to end my short life. I saw Addeline and my heart leaped when I caught sight of her. She was up in the gallery gripping the rail so hard her knuckles showed through like white marble. She was dressed as a boy, but I would know her anywhere.

She never even looked down at me once. And just thinking about it now is bringing me close to tears . . .

'So if you don't tell me, lad, who'll ever know?' The ordinary's rough voice brought me back out of my dream. He took out his pen.

'Ah, go on then, son – it's a good tale, I'll warrant! And you should hear the ones they've made up about you already.'

'Oh?' I said, trying to feign disinterest, but I knew enough about people to know he knew he had me hooked. 'What *do* they say about me?'

'They say the boat was magicked away by witchcraft! They say you're too clever to be a boy, that you're a man who never growed, and that you had a sack of gold and you would walk about the streets by St Dunstan's throwing money in the air for poor children to catch.'

'Hah!' I would have folded my arms but the chains

were so damn short they didn't allow for it. 'That was me and Addy once – we had so much cash in our pockets it was weighing us down. And we had to run so fast . . .' I shook my head remembering.

'They say you can escape from any lock save ones blessed by a bishop, and the vanished ship sails back and forth between the Indies and Africa freeing slaves and causing pain for the planters!'

I smiled. 'Is that all?'

'And they say you're an angel that fell down into hell. Oh, that's on account of your smooth words and your kind eyes and your infernal skin.'

'My skin is far from infernal!' I protested. 'It's been my living every one of my thirteen years! I'm as proud of my colour as the peacock is of his feathers!' I said. 'Go on. Write that down to start.'

'So you'll talk?'

I took a deep sigh. That was a big mistake because of the smell. The odour of the seven others who were to hang with me tomorrow and the filth of us all packed together in sweat and grime filled my insides. It took me a long time to ready myself. How would I start? My education in crime in the Liberty of the Fleet, in and out of the Nest of Vipers, learning to pick a lock and watching Addy turn over country gentlemen in Smithfield playing find the lady?

Or the crime I was set to give my life for – the most incredible scam ever laid by man or woman, the secret of the *Favourite*? I smiled to myself. I'd keep some of my secrets a little longer.

Anyway, if I tried telling all, we'd run out of time and I would be swinging in the wind, dancing the devil's own jig on the end of a noose. There was so much to tell . . . Arabella playing the fine lady, me the page done up like the Queen's Own dog's dinner? Or when I was younger, when Mother Hopkins sold me so many times over I almost forgot my own name! And we played so many lays over so many years – to be straight with you it was just like any other job of work. But there were one or two times . . . one or two marks who deserved absolutely everything they got. And, yes, one family stands out. So venal and so stupid that we took them several times. And in the end they were my own downfall – the Walkers of Greenwich.

Yes, I'll start there. And it was how we first met Sam Caesar. He's one of the best chairmen in town now, as it goes. Him and Jack Godwin rule Leicester Fields; they can carry you, in their sedan chair, from Covent Garden to St James's in half the time you'd make with a carriage and pair. I only wish they were waiting for me now, outside, and I could slip my chains, and melt into the walls and be away.

That's not going to happen. The beak's been so afraid of my escape again, I'm shackled and trussed like a pheasant in a butcher's window.

I look at the Newgate ordinary. He's so dirty you can only just make out his chaplain's collar. He's greedy for my words because to him they're solid old gory. Old gory? Blood-and-bread, quids, love-of-my-life, rhino, money. The root of all evil and the staff of life. I make him promise he'll use some of the cash he'll make to save my body from the surgeon's knife. Then I begin.

'So, here they are,' I say. 'The last words of Cato Hopkins, boy criminal. Who only ever robbed those that were so greedy as to want more. Who only ever tried to share about the wealth of those that are fat with goods and silks and food—'

'Hold on!' the ordinary says. 'Slow down, for the sake of my quill!'

'It was like this. It was my eighth year or so, and we was living above the pub, the Nest of Vipers. Trade was slow and the only regular money in was from Bella's job at Two Crows coffee shop and whatever me and Addy brought in from the street. Then this boy walks in – well, he looked like a man; he was the size of a man. It was Sam Caesar, fifteen but more than fully grown. He was bleeding from a knock on his head and he was so desperate it took more than Mother Hopkins's soft words and a cup of ale to quieten him down.

'"I need help," he said.

'Mother Hopkins dabbed away the blood and said, slow and not interested, like, "I can see that, my lad. Now, what is it you think we can do for you?"

'He told us then about his owner, man name of Captain Walker, lived over Greenwich in one of them big new houses, stuffed to the gills with paintings and silver. Mother Hopkins's ears pricked up at this. But we'd already guessed as much for the poor chap was wearing one of them god-awful silver collars that the rich put their slaves in. Have you seen them? Bet you've never worn one! They're the devil and that's the truth, heavy as lead and there's nothing so likely to make you feel like a dog as wearing one of them. Sam's collar read: *SAM, Capt. Walker's Negro. Please return to Croom's Hill, Greenwich*, in that curly writing. I felt a deal of pity for the boy just for that.

'Sam Caesar said he'd heard there was folk here who knew how to turn situations around, and his was a situation so parlous that he could not imagine any way out.

'Bella put another cup of ale in front of the boy and smiled at him. If she hadn't have been seeing Jack Goodwin she'd have set her cap at him, I'm sure of it: Sam Caesar was fine looking – at least he would be when the gash on his head was cleaned up.

'Turned out Captain Walker had brought our Sam over from Jamaica when he was a lad. Captain Walker wasn't just a sea captain, oh no. He had a deal of estates in Jamaica producing sugar and rum. Owned hundreds of slaves, Sam said; still owned his mother, Juno. And she'd been a favourite with the captain, so favourite that Sam had a lighter skin than his mother, if you get my meaning. So favourite that she'd begged the captain to take Sam to London and give him some kind of education. So Sam had come over with the captain and grown up in Greenwich as their page; wearing one of them flashy outfits with slippers with those curly toes and a turban. Never learned nothing but serving chocolate and tea to visiting ladies, mind. Then a few years ago he'd grown too big for that lay and they used him as a footman. But the captain never liked him: any excuse and he'd get a clout like the one he was wearing that day. And then he hears the captain's only gone and sold him to a mate and is having him shipped back to Jamaica on the *Retort* to be a field hand!

'I knew then why he trembled so. If you ever heard the old men in St Giles, talking about life in the Indies, it would make your hair turn white. Floggings so hard flesh hangs in red ribbons from a man's back. Men, women and children worked until they break; arms, ears, tongues cut off! Death is your only friend out there, I've heard say, because it's a sleep you never have to wake from.

'"He wants to disappear," I said, already wanting to help.

'But Mother Hopkins shot me a "Shut up" look. "He's not free, Cato, not like you!" she said. "Someone'll buy him, sell him, in two shakes of a lamb's tail. He's not free, Cato." She said it again.

'I said nothing. Mother Hopkins was always right. Whenever I was sold, usually in some such town as Nottingham or Derby or Bedford – once as far as Chester – we were up and had a distance of twenty miles between ourselves and my newest masters before they realized I had gone. And if anyone *was* foolish enough to come after me, Mother Hopkins had a tame lawyer – Mr De Souza in the Strand –

with enough writs to confuse and confound our enemies. And failing that, Jack and Sam, who have more muscle than most . . .

'Anyway,' I said to the ordinary, 'back to the track of my tale. Sam fair jumped up out of his seat at the mention of liberty.

'"Freedom!" he said. "Captain Walker promised my mother he'd make me a free man. I was there when he made the promise, and she gave him a letter! She put it into his hand the day I left. He denies it all of course, says my mother could hardly speak English let alone read and write. They never bothered teaching me so I can't tell. I found a bundle of letters but they all look the same, black lines on white paper, like the trails of ants or some such."

'Mother Hopkins thought a long minute. "So this man owes you at least your freedom?"

'Sam nodded.

'"And he has plenty of rhino about the house?" she said.

'Sam looked blank.

'"Rhino, ready money, cash?" Mother Hopkins said.

'Sam nodded again. "His wife is most fond of the cards, though she loses as often as she wins, and she has jewellery too – they have so much money from the backs of their slaves, who work day and night for them but are paid nothing!" Sam was so angry when he spoke it was hard for him to keep still. "But whatever plans you make, it must be soon. I am to leave his household in a fortnight, and go to Rotherhithe, where the boat will be loaded."

'Now, Mother Hopkins seems to sit at the heart of a web that stretches all over the city. She had Addy go over to Greenwich to check out the gaff, and Bella went to some rather genteel card games with her pockets full of flummery – fake cash to you – where she picked up a not inconsiderable amount of info. I was to be the inside man, although as I was just eight I suppose you would say "boy". But I had done the job so many times before.

'Bella let slip there was a sale in Long Acre. Mother Hopkins had the bills produced: *For sale:*

Cato, a most pleasant and agreeable negro boy. Of only six years of age (I know, I was eight – never believe any advertisements ever), *new from the jungles of Zanzibar, he is a mute, having been raised by leopards!* (What did I say about advertisements?)

'Mother Hopkins knew it would hook the captain's wife. Sam had told us she was looking for a new page, and that she wanted one more exotic and more mysterious than Mrs Gerald's boy, of whom it was said – mostly by Mrs Gerald herself – that he had been found floating in the Indian Ocean in a giant shell.

'I always hated the sales. We had played this game so many times before, I the slave, sold by Mother Hopkins, over and over all around the country, and I never stayed in any of them fine houses longer than a fortnight – there's another hundred more tales for you, sir! I know, I know, I must keep to one story at a time.

'So, even though in my heart of hearts I knew I would be back at the Nest of Vipers within the week, there was something about the saleroom that made my eye moisten and my lip tremble every single time. Mother Hopkins encouraged this as she said it made a good spectacle.

'Captain Walker was a nasty piece – I could tell this by the way he checked my teeth as if I was a horse, prodding around inside my mouth so hard I could not help but flinch. I was much minded to bite off his fingers, but Mother Hopkins fixed me with her evil eye.

'He paid five guineas for me, then he took me straightway by boat to Greenwich, and Addeline was right: the house was one of those big show-off white-icing affairs.

'It is strange that people who wouldn't dream of walking through the streets with their money hanging out of their pockets are more than happy to advertise their wealth through clothes or carriages or houses. The house gleamed like a beacon to the cracksmen of London, and I thought they would have fine pickings here.

'My jaw fairly dropped inside the house. Paintings – ships and portraits mostly – I would ignore the portraits; they never sold – and one of horses in the modern style that Mother Hopkins would be most pleased with. I reminded myself to keep my hands hard in my pockets, for our spoils were to be human rather than material.

'Then Mrs Walker comes down the stairs clapping her hands and saying, "Oh! Oh! He is a darling, and he is mute, John? Such a fetching affectation!"

'Then the captain says to her, "He'll do – at least he'll be quiet. How is Elizabeth? Did she like the Spencer lad?"

'The missus says, "Oh yes, John, she's quite taken with the diamond necklace he bought her. And all that dreadful business can be forgotten. They're coming round for tea this afternoon and now little Sam here can do the honours in his fine suit." She clapped her hands together again. "What a pet!" and then chucks me under the chin, and says to me very slowly, as if she reckons I can't speak the Queen's English, "You'll be our Sam now – the name's on the collar and we're not about to change it. We've always had a Sam here and we always will." She leans down to me and her eyes are pale and watery and she says, "You'll find Greenwich a deal of difference to the jungle, little Sam." I have to bite my tongue hard to stop myself laughing out loud. And she leads me away to put on the threads I am to spend my working week in.

'The suit was brocade, navy blue and also heavy as lead, and the turban too big. Mendes, the cove that Mother Hopkins sells old threads to, would give a pretty penny for the lot but they didn't half itch. And the collar! Wouldn't you know it is the same one Sam had been wearing the week before, so it is far too big and digs into my shoulders a good deal.

'At least I am right good at pouring chocolate from a silver pot. Mother Hopkins has taught me well. And I see the daughter, Miss Elizabeth – well, I see her sparklers, which are as beautiful as she is, only more honest looking, and I'm so busy thinking about how Mother Hopkins would die of delight if she could see that necklace that I forget Mistress Spencer and her lumpy son.

'"Sam!" Mistress Walker claps her hands. I did

nothing for a long minute on account of having forgotten I was now Sam and not Cato. "Sam, our guests!" Then she says to Mistress Spencer, "He is newly come from Africa, directly from the jungle . . . he doesn't speak a word . . ." She looked at me with mock pity. "Captain Walker says he is the son of a prince and was brought up by leopards!"

'I stood up straight. I would have laughed if Miss Elizabeth hadn't been pinching me hard – to see if I'll squeal, I reckoned. I had to feel pity for the girl; there she was being lined up for the Spencer boy, just like me at the auction. I looked hard at him: it would not be a barrel of laughs being married to him. But at least her collar was made of diamonds, and she did not seem to mind. I think she was set on his fortune, not on his looks or manners, and in view of her pinching, her manners were of the same rank as his.

'Sam had been put to work in the garden and bade not to leave the house or grounds. I could see him through the window turning over the cold earth. He eats with us in the kitchen, but as I am supposed to be mute, nothing is ever said. He is nervous, though, I can tell.

'At night I sleep down in the kitchen and talk to Sam then. I spring the lock on my collar (they insist I sleep in it!) and resolve to take Sam's letter. I tiptoe back up the stairs to the study. The lock is feeble and the door opens easily, as does the bureau.

'Inside, however, there are so many letters I am losing all faith that I will find it – letters from banks and ship's companies, sums of money flying back and forth across various oceans and through various banks. But eventually I come across the very same. It is *"written on behalf of a Mistress Juno Walker of Spanish Town, Jamaica, by the Reverend Butler"*. Juno – I thinks to myself – Sam's mother. I know the fashion for giving us darker-skinned people such fanciful names as have come out of legends or history – for example, Cato is not – as Addeline would tease me – the king of Cats but the finest Roman that ever lived. Although as you see, sir, I am not myself a Roman, and neither, I expect, was this Juno, who had a priest write for her and, by her

162

words, beg that her son should be treated better than she was. And Walker? Well, don't most slaves wear their master's names whether or not they wish to?

'Back to the letter . . . the writing is faded and old. I held it up to the window where the moonlight streams in over Greenwich Park and thanked Mother Hopkins for teaching me the reading as I reckons that sometimes it is more valuable and just as useful as the best set of lock picks money can buy.

'The next few days dragged as slow as the Cheapside night watchman, and he has such a limp as he can hardly make it down St Paul's yard. The household was busy enough, Captain Walker with his shareholdings, Mistress and Miss Walker with the wedding that had been brokered with the Spencer family. I stood in the corner of the drawing room with my silver tray saying nothing. They treated me much as they would a lap dog: from the mistress it was soft words, from Miss Elizabeth pinches and from the captain slaps and kicks. I felt sorry for Sam having such a father and was glad I had none. I was looking forward to the day I could walk out of their house and take off the damnable silver collar for good. I was only sorry I wouldn't see the look on the captain's face when he realized what was happening.

'I busied myself with secreting little things they wouldn't miss: a hatpin with a pearl, a couple of silver spoons and the captain's seal that he used for business correspondence. I tossed them all over the wall when I knew Addy was waiting by the park, as a little taster. I put the letter over too, knowing Mother Hopkins would make the best use of it and knowing Sam would like to see his mother's letter when this was all over.

'The captain noticed his seal gone that evening; he was like an ox that's been driven wild at Smithfield by the 'prentices, and made the same amount of noise and mess, throwing his papers about and bellowing. The mistress was obviously well used to this behaviour. She told him it had probably just been misplaced, or worst of all fallen down between the boards, and not to go so red in the face. His anxiety would be the death of him, she said, and made Miss

Elizabeth sing to soothe him, which I think only made him worse.

'That night Sam came to me where I slept in the kitchen. He was almost mad with worry and fear.

'"They are coming for me in the morning, Cato! And I have seen no progress! I can wait no longer. I will run tonight – you can open the front door for me and I can take a place on a boat."

'I begged him not to go: Captain Walker would know all the boats this side of the river and probably half the ones on the north side.

'"Sam, please! You must trust Mother Hopkins. Captain Walker will put a price on your head if you run, and any boatman will turn you over soon as look at you!"

'"You are but a baby who knows nothing!" he said, and I went to speak again, but Mrs Leppings the cook came to see what the noise was.

'I stayed up all night in case I heard him try to leave. I was so vexed I bit my fingernails to the quick imagining Sam chained to the mast of a boat in the Thames and – in my worst nightmares –

me alongside him sailing for the plantations.

'In the morning the doorbell sounded early, eight thirty, and Sam was shaking. But it was a messenger from the bank, a boy dressed in the livery of the Commonwealth and Indies Trading Bank. A slight and slender boy, but the captain let him in and the boy winked at me and I had to keep my face straight because Addeline made such a very convincing boy.

'She asked for the captain's signature and waited while he signed and sealed (with his second best seal) various letters. Then the messenger boy was gone.

'So, when (I imagine) the Mistress Walker called for her little Sam to pour chocolate that morning at eleven, she called for ever, louder and louder and longer and longer, until she must have been quite red in the face. Sam and I had slipped out of the back door into the street, where Mother Hopkins and Bella waited with a change of clothes for me and Sam Caesar's certificate of freedom, signed and sealed that morning by the captain himself.

'And by eleven o'clock me and Sam were sat snug in the upstairs room at the Nest of Vipers, Mother Hopkins counting the cash she'd made from selling my collar and clothes, Addy still dressed as a boy, her eyes saucer-wide as I told her about the house and the diamonds.

'I read Sam the letter from his mother, her tender words hoping her son would find his freedom in England, but Sam snatched it away, pretending the tears I could see so plain were provoked by nothing but a bit of dust.

'Oh, Sam can read himself now – Bella taught him, and Mother Hopkins bought the fine sedan chair he runs with Jack Godwin – you must have seen them in all their wigs and livery; you won't find sharper pair of young men!

'I had hoped, one day' – I sighed and shifted on the hard stone floor – 'I would be like Sam . . .'

I tried to stretch – my wrists were raw and oozing under the shackles – and I yawned, making the ordinary yawn too. He was still scratching away with his quill. Then, when I spoke no more, the ordinary looked up from his scribbling and said, 'Was that the end of it? Didn't the captain come after you? What about the sparklers – the diamonds? I thought you were going to pocket them? And how does this relate to the *Favourite*? Was that not tied into the Walkers? Wasn't he the man in court done up in naval rig?'

'Perhaps,' I said. 'And we had his seal, remember, and a lot more besides. And the sparklers . . . well, that'll be another story . . .'

I could tell from the tone of his voice that the ordinary fair drooled to hear more. Outside the watchman called the hour for five o'clock. I had so little time . . .

We'd be leaving at eleven for the drive to Tyburn along the Oxford Road and then the hanging, my hanging, at noon.

I sighed. Only seven more hours.

PART FOUR

TOWARDS FREEDOM

GARY PAULSEN

Extract from:

Nightjohn

My life is short, but some live long and the one
thing we know, short or long – it's wrong to run. Not
wrong because it's wrong. But wrong because
nobody ever gets away.

I've seen two to try it. Both men. One was an old
man named Jim who just couldn't take no more and
one night he up and cut.

They set after him the next morning with dogs.
Only the master, he don't only go his ownself
but took five or six field hands with him to see

so they can carry what they see back to tell us.

The dogs be mean. He feeds them things to make them mean. Blood things. Sometimes he'll take them to the fields and should a man or woman work a little behind the others, or behind the best man, who is whipped to speed – why, he sets the dogs on the slow one. And he don't pull them off right away, neither. Lets them go until they taste blood and want more of it.

They's mean, the dogs. They's big and red with tight hair and heads like hogs and mean as Waller his ownself. He keeps them in a stone pen by the side of the horse barn and they slobber and chew at the gate each time we walk by. Dirt mean.

Jim, he ran at night too but it didn't help. The field hands told us later. He cut and ran down to the river, ran in the water for a goodly distance, then on the top of a fence rail for as long as the fence ran and then dropped to the ground and just moved.

The dogs followed him all the way. The hands said that one dog even got up and ran on the top rail of the fence. Only took half a day and they caught Jim.

The last bit, when he heard the dogs singing him, baying on him, Jim climbed a tree. Problem was, the tree wasn't higher than he could reach, nearly, and as high as he got, the bottom of him hung down where the dogs could reach him.

The master set the dogs on him and they tore and ripped what they could reach until there wasn't any meat on Jim's legs or bottom. The dogs ripped it all off, to hang in shreds. The field hands say he still didn't let go, nor never did. Even when he was dead his hands didn't let go and the master made the field hands leave him there. They's some wanted to take Jim down and bury him but he made them to leave him that way, hanging by his hands in the tree, for the birds to eat.

Second man was young. Name of Pawley. He wasn't a big enough hand to be allowed to be a breeder in the quarters and so he went to looking. He snucked away and met a girl at a plantation down the road a piece and they sat in the moonlight with each other some nights. Pawley he made it back before wake-up time every night but one, the last one. He fell asleep in his girl's arms, fell asleep in the moonlight.

So they from the white house set out with the dogs and Pawley he didn't run, or try to get away. He was on his way home but they let the dogs to have him anyway, tear him up to bleed but not kill him. Then the master he tied him down and cut him like he did the cattle so he wouldn't run to girls no more, but the cut went wrong and Pawley he laid all night and bled to death without ever making a sound in the corner of the quarters.

So don't nobody run. Besides, I don't think there's a place to run to. I heard talk once of some land, some land north but it's far away and it was only talk. Not something to know. Just something to hear. Like birds singing, the talk of the land north, or the wind in the trees.

But Alice cut and run that night.

She didn't get far. Down to the river and then sideways some. Her back was still ripped and sore and she must have moved slow. She might have kept moving all night but hadn't gone more than to the other end of the cotton fields – an easy small walk. Then she pulled herself under some brambles and was there when they found her.

He let the dogs to have her.

Didn't matter what she'd gone through, or that her thinking wasn't working right. The field hands with him told us he smiled his big white smile like the big white house, pale maggot white like his skin smile and let the dogs to have her. She didn't fight them or try to get away and they just tore at her. Tore at her until her whole front was torn and gone and she was bleeding from the chest.

She didn't die.

Alice be too tough for her ownself good. She didn't die and he made the hands to carry her back and put her in the quarters. Mammy sewed up what she could with canvas thread and greased and patched and she lived.

She be like Pawley. She didn't make sounds even while mammy was pulling at the torn flaps of skin and sewing them on her chest. Not a sound. Just stared and stared at the wall.

That night John called to me as he came past where

I was trying to sleep.

'Tobacco girl – time for another letter.'

I had been all day helping mammy and was tired and sad for Alice, how she be at the other end of the quarters, but I went just the same. I still had two letters coming for that first pinch of tobacco.

He was sitting on his heels in the open doorway.

I squatted next to him. 'What's the next one?'

He used a stick with a sharpened end on it and wiggled in the dirt two half circles:

B

'Bee,' he said. 'It be B.'

'That sounds crazy . . .'

'That's how you say the letter. *B*. It's for *behh* or *be* or *buh* or *boo*. That's how a *B* looks and how you make the sound.'

I made it sound in my mouth, whispering. 'So where's the bottom to it?'

'I swear – you always want to know the bottom to things. Here, here it is. It sits on itself this way, facing so the two round places push to the front.'

Suddenly he's gone. One second he's there, the next he's slammed sideways and gone.

'What in the *hell* are you doing to her?'

Mammy was standing there, big and black and tall in the moonlight. 'What you doing to this girl?'

She had come from the side and fetched John such a blow on his head that it knocked him back into the wall and on his back.

He came up quick and didn't cower none.

'Nothing. Not like you think. I'm teaching her to read.'

'That's what I mean,' mammy said. 'What in the *hell* are you doing? Don't you know what they do to her if they find her trying to read? We already got one girl tore to pieces by the whip and the dogs. We don't need two.'

I'd been quiet all this time, watching. Didn't seem so bad, what he was doing. Teaching me a few letters to know. Maybe a word or two. So I said it. 'Doesn't seem so bad—'

'*Bad*?' Then she hissed like a snake. 'Child, they'll

177

cut your thumbs off if you learn to read. They'll whip you until your back looks knitted – until it looks like his back.' She pointed to John, big old finger. 'Is that how you got whipped?'

He shook his head. 'I ran.'

'And got caught.'

'Not the first time.'

She waited. I waited.

'First time I ran I got clean away. I went north, all the way. I was free.'

I'd never heard such a thing. We couldn't even talk about being free. And here was a man said he had been free by running north. I thought, How can that be?

'You ran and got away?' mammy asked.

'I did.'

'You ran until you were clean away?'

'I did.'

'And you came *back*?'

'I did.'

'Why?'

He sighed and it sounded like his voice, like his

laugh. Low and way off thunder. It made me think he was going to promise something, the way thunder promises rain. 'For this.'

'What you mean – this?'

'To teach reading.'

It's never quiet in the quarters. During the day the young ones run and scrabble and fight or cry and they's always a gaggle of them. At night everybody be sleeping. But not quiet. Alice, she's quiet. But they's some of them to cry. New workers who are just old enough to be working in the fields cry sometimes in their sleep. They hurt and their hands bleed and pain them from new blisters that break and break again. Old workers cry because they're old and getting to the end and have old pain. Same pain, young and old. Some snore. Others just breathe loud.

It's a long building and dark except for the light coming in the door and the small windows, but it's never quiet. Not even at night.

Now it seemed quiet. Mammy she looked down at John. Didn't say nothing for a long time. Just looked.

I had to think to hear the breathing, night sounds. Finally mammy talks. Her voice is soft. 'You came back to teach reading?'

John nodded. 'That's half of it.'

'What's the other half?'

'Writing.' He smiled. 'Course, I wasn't going to get caught. I had in mind moving, moving around. Teaching a little here, a little there. Going to do hidey-schools. But I got slow and they got fast and some crackers caught me in the woods. They were hunting bear, but the dogs came on me instead and I took to a tree and they got me.'

Another long quiet. Way off, down by the river, I heard the sound of a night-bird. Singing for day. Soon the sun would come.

'Why does it matter?' Mammy leaned against the wall. She had one hand on the logs, one on her cheek. Tired. 'Why do that to these young ones? To Sarny here. If they learn to read—'

'And write.'

'And write, it's just grief for them. Longtime grief. They find what they don't have, can't have. It ain't good to know that. It eats at you then – to know it and not have it.'

'They have to be able to write,' John said. Voice pushing. He stood and reached out one hand with long fingers and touched mammy on the forehead. It was almost like he be kissing her with his fingers. Soft. Touch like black cotton in the dark. 'They have to read and write. We all have to read and write so we can write about this – what they doing to us. It has to be written.'

Mammy she turned and went back to her mat on the floor. Moving quiet, not looking back. She settled next to the young ones and John he turned to me and he say:

'Next is *C*.'

GRACE NICHOLS

The People Could Fly

**This poem is based on an old African belief that
if you declined to eat salt, then your soul would grow
light enough to fly back to Africa.**

The people could fly –
See them rise up, a cloud of locusts
or more a host of scarecrows in suneye?
Wind flapping against their
sunworn dresses and tattered shirt-coats

This brethren who lived a life
of saltless endurance.
No slave-food – saltbeef, saltfish,
to blight their blood or mock the freedom,
the heady helium gathering slowly in their veins.

How closely they guarded their levitational-mystery
How calmly they carried out their earthly duties

And now it's lift-off time –
See them making for the
green open hilltops
with nothing but their faith
and their corncobs?

Hear them singing; One bright morning
when my work is over I will fly away home . . .

The people could fly.
Look! Look, how they coming, Africa!
'Goodbye plantation goodbye.'

MALORIE BLACKMAN

North

'That child of yours able to breed yet?'

'No, sir.'

'You sure? She started her monthlies?'

'No, sir.' Mama shook her head. 'She's only a baby.'

Best Friend grabbed at my face with one of his pudgy, doughy hands. He squeezed my cheeks together until my eyes started to water. He turned my face this way and that as he looked me up and down.

'She ain't no baby.' Best Friend pushed me away and wiped his hand on his waistcoat. 'The minute she's old enough to breed, I've got someone ready to buy her.'

'Mama—'

'Hush, child.' Mama quietened me down at once.

I glared up at Best Friend. How could he take me from my mama? How would he feel if someone took his own daughter Amelia away from him? But as far as Best Friend and all the other whites up at the house were concerned, us slaves didn't have no feelings. I hated him so much that sometimes I thought I'd fill up the whole world with hate.

Best Friend's eyes began to narrow as he looked at me and I knew my face was showing too much. I blanked my expression and looked down at the dirt.

'I want to know the moment she's got the curse. D'you hear, Abby?'

'Yes, sir,' Mama replied.

Best Friend stomped back to the house. Mama had sure got his name right. He was the best friend of the Devil and no mistake. I waited until he was safely in the house before turning round.

'Mama, you're not going to let him sell me, are you? You can't.'

Mama carried on staring up at the house.

'Mama?'

'Hush, child. Come along now. We've got work to do and I don't fancy no back-whipping just 'cause you've got it in your head to ask questions.'

'I won't go. I won't. He can't make me,' I shouted.

'Child, hold your noise,' Mama warned.

'I won't go, d'you hear? And if you let him take me then you're . . . you're nothing but a coward and a—'

Mama slapped me so hard, my head snapped back.

'That's enough of your foolishness,' she hissed. 'Now get back to work on those vegetables, you hear?'

Mama moved off towards the side of the house. Tears swam into my eyes and down my cheeks as I watched her move away. And just at that moment, I hated her. I hated her for giving in, for saying 'Yes, sir' and 'No, sir' all the time. I hated her for being a slave. I hated her because I was her daughter and that made me a slave too and I would've chosen to be any number of other things – even Best Friend's worst kept dog – before I was a slave.

I went to work tending to the vegetables, wondering what I should do. Best Friend didn't know it yet but I was already seeing the curse. I'd had the curse for almost three months now. It was only a matter of time before he got to find out and then I'd be sold to the highest bidder faster than I could spit. But what could I do? As I dug around the carrots and potatoes, I turned over and over in my mind all the things I could do to get away. I turned my head this way and that, wondering which way I'd have to go to be free. Which was the right direction? All the ways looked the same. There were no paths leading away. Each road just led back to Best Friend's door.

A cool, hard hand clamped over my mouth. My eyes opened that same second.

'Hhmmm! Ugghh!' I struggled against the hand. My hands flew upwards to pull it off my mouth.

'Shush!' Mama's voice barely a whisper. 'Shush! We're going north.'

We're going north.

You can have no idea what those few words did

to me. I was that instant awake, as if a bucket of winter water had been tipped all over me. I was scared. More than scared. Terrified. But I was happy. Fiercely, raging happy. We were leaving. We were going to run away. And where were we going?

North.

North meant freedom. North was the closest thing on God's earth to Heaven. My eyes were getting used to the moonlit darkness. I smiled at Mama. She didn't smile back. Instead her eyes burned into mine, shining hot and bright as the very sun itself.

Mama took hold of my hand as I sat up and we tiptoed past the others in our shack who lay on sacking on the floor. I could hear folks sighing and some were even crying in their sleep. As we approached, Old John, who lay in the middle of the shack, started coughing, that terrible hacking, bone-shaking cough of his. I'm used to him coughing himself to sleep and then coughing himself awake again, but at that moment I was terrified he was going to wake up the whole world. Mama led the way towards the door. Old John hacked so bad, he started to sit up. Mama froze, her grip on my hand tightening. I didn't even dare to breathe. Old John didn't hold with folks running off. He said it was useless, a waste of time and just made life harder for everyone else.

As if life could get any harder.

Old John gave one final cough and collapsed back down onto his bedding. Immediately Mama pulled me towards the door. I almost stepped on Old John's foot – more in spite than anything else – but I wanted to go north more than I wanted to get back at him for almost ruining our escape.

At last we were at the door. Mama opened it and for once it didn't squeak.

'Mama . . . ?'

'I oiled it. Shush!'

And then we were outside. In the warm, night-time air. It had never felt so good on my face. The full moon shone like new money, but beneath the trees, where the moonlight didn't reach, there was pure darkness. I mean, darkness thick enough to almost drink.

'Sit.' Mama pushed down on one of my shoulders.

I sat down with a bump. After another quick glance

around, then up at the house, Mama dug into her sack and took out two rolled-up squares of rawhide and tied them to my feet using some rope. There was something slippy in the raw hide that made my toes curl. Then Mama sat and tied two larger squares of rawhide onto her own feet. She jumped up, pulling me up after her. Across the way I could see Best Friend's house. A single light shone in an upstairs window. Mama looked at it too, a cold, hard look on her face. She pulled me in the opposite direction, towards the trees. And we started running.

We ran and ran and ran until I thought I was going to throw up my whole insides all over my rawhide shoes.

'Mama, can we stop?' I panted.

'No, child. Not yet.'

We ran and ran and ran some more. My legs felt burning hot, melting my bones away to nothing.

'Mama, I need to stop. My legs hurt. My chest is burning.'

'No, child. Not yet.'

We ran until I fell to the ground, weeping.

'Mama, I can't go on no more. I can't.'

Mama squatted down in front of me, cupping my face in both her hands. 'Child, we'll rest for five minutes then we must keep moving. We have a long way to go before we reach the Ohio River.'

'And what happens then?'

'We cross the river and then we'll be north. Not north where we'll be free, but north where we should be safe. And then we'll just keep going north until we're free as the wind.'

I rubbed the rawhide covering my feet. The soles of my feet felt slippery and sore.

'What's in this rawhide, Mama?'

'Lard, pepper and some strong-smelling herbs.'

'Why?'

'To throw off the dogs. The minute Best Friend finds out we've gone, he'll be after us with every dog he's got.'

'It ain't right to set dogs on people.' I shook my head.

'Child, a lot of things in this world ain't right. You change them and fix them or you just put up with them.'

'We can't change anything, Mama. We're just slaves.'

'Uh-uh! No!' Mama shook her head. 'Just 'cause white folks say we're only fit to be slaves don't make it so – don't make it true.'

'Maybe we're fixing things by . . . by running away?'

'Maybe we are at that.' A trace of a smile played across Mama's face.

I bowed my head and sighed. 'I'm sorry for what I said this afternoon. I didn't mean it.'

'I know that.' Mama sat next to me on the dry, cool ground and gathered me into her arms. 'And I'm sorry I slapped you. But I think I was so angry 'cause I thought maybe you was right.'

I was shocked. 'You ain't no coward, Mama. The Devil's Best Friend is the coward, whipping us and starving us and worse. He ain't no kind of man. Not as I would describe it, anyways.'

Mama laughed softly. 'Child, the things you come out with.'

'Amelia taught me some things.' I lowered my

voice. 'Mama, Amelia taught me my letters and numbers and some words.'

Mama stared at me, her face bathed in the silver moonlight, shining through the trees. 'Did she now . . .'

'That's until she started listening to Best Friend and decided I wasn't fit to spit on,' I sighed.

'So you can read and write?'

'Some.'

'How come you never told me before?'

'I thought you might get mad at me,' I admitted.

'Well, I'm glad you had sense enough to hide it. The Devil's Best Friend would've chopped off your hands for sure if he thought you could write letters and words.'

And weren't that the truth. Best Friend would've probably done something to my eyes as well to make sure I couldn't read no more either. That was the kind of less-than-human he was.

Mama got to her feet, pulling me up after her. 'Come on, child. We still have a long, long way to go.'

My heart had only just stopped jumping about in

my chest and now here we were, running again.

'Mama, are we running 'cause of me?'

Mama slowed at that. Turning to me, she said, 'I wanted to run after you was born. I didn't want another child of mine to be a slave, but your daddy said we should stay together. If we ran and got caught . . . So I stayed and one winter turned into two and two turned into three. And your daddy was sold away and I told myself that I could bear that if I had you. But I'm not letting Best Friend sell you. I'm not letting you grow up like me. You're much too precious to me to let that happen to you.'

I smiled. 'I love you too, Mama.'

Mama hugged me harder than hard, just for an instant. But then it was over.

'Now that's enough talk.' She frowned. 'We have to save our breath for running.'

And we were off again. We ran. But my steps seemed lighter and my heart was not quite so heavy. Not quite. We were going north.

One day later, it wasn't an adventure any more. The

adventure side of things had left a long time ago. A lifetime ago. Every owl's hoot, every cracking twig, every shuffle and rustle and murmur put my heart clean up in my mouth. The thrilling, exciting part about running away had faded to nothing. I was scared to death. Scared so I couldn't even summon up enough spit in my bone-dry mouth to swallow. Best Friend was sure to have summoned up all the help he could to track us down. And we didn't seem to be making much progress. We stuck to the trees for as long as we could and only travelled at night, hiding during the day, but the night didn't last long. Night was unbearably short. All the field slaves used to say that when they came back to the slave shack, dragging their feet and hanging their heads with exhaustion, almost too tired to eat what little there was. They'd just fall onto their sacking, wishing the night was twice as long as it was – the way we all did. I knew Mama and I were lucky. We were house slaves. We had it bad enough, but the field slaves had it much worse. But now that Mama and me were on the run, the night time seemed to pass in the blink of an eye.

Mama and I were hiding high up in a tree. In the distance I was sure I could hear dogs barking. I used my hand to wipe the sweat off my forehead. Horrified, I imagined Best Friend and his men standing under the tree, realizing why it was raining from the tree and nowhere else. I looked up at Mama.

She smiled at me and whispered, 'Don't worry, child. Even if I don't make it, you surely will.'

'I want to go north with you, Mama,' I protested.

'And you will, honey. But maybe you'll get there before me. If that happens then I'll be along later – I promise.'

'What do we do now?'

'We wait for the night to come,' Mama said softly. 'I reckon in a few more days we'll reach the Ohio River.'

'I'm hungry.' I pressed my hands over my stomach, which was rumbling.

Mama dug into her brown sack and took out a red apple. Handing it down to me, she warned, 'Give me the core when you've finished. We don't need to leave behind no clues to help them find us.'

I began to eat the apple the way I always did, with big fat bites.

'Slow, little nibbles,' Mama urged. 'There's not much food left. Make it last.'

'D'you want some, Mama?'

Mama shook her head. It occurred to me that I hadn't seen Mama eat very much of anything since we'd started running.

'Aren't you hungry?'

'Yes, but not for food,' Mama whispered. 'I'm hungry to see my daughter free. I'm hungry to keep one of my children by my side. That no-kind-of-man Best Friend has already sold three of my children away from me – like I was a rock or a stone with no feelings.'

'I have brothers and sisters?' I stared at her. 'I never knew that.'

'What was the use in telling you? We neither of us are ever going to see them again. They've gone and that's that. But I won't let them take you away from me. I won't.'

'How many brothers do I have? How many sisters? What are their names? Where are they—?'

'Child, I don't want to hear another word about them, d'you hear? I don't know where they are. I try not to think about them. It tears up my heart to think about them. So not another word.'

Mama closed her eyes and turned her head. There were so many things I wanted to ask her but I didn't speak. I didn't even open my mouth. I suddenly had brothers and sisters and not knowing any of them hurt. It hurt something fierce. I tried and tried but I just didn't understand what made Best Friend and others like him hate us so much. And they must surely hate us to trample us into the dirt the way they did. Who made the rule that we were less than them because of the colour of our skin? Was it written down somewhere? In what book? And who wrote it? I tried and tried but I just couldn't figure it out.

Mama and I both sat in silence for a long time. Mama's eyes were clouded over, like she was in pain but doing her best not to scream out. I wanted to do something to cheer her – but how, when I didn't feel cheered myself?

'What else is in the sack, Mama?'

'A few berries, some bread and a knife in case we're lucky enough to catch a rabbit or some fish.'

I nodded but didn't reply. The knife was to protect us. I'm not stupid. I knew that much. After all, when would we have time for skinning and cleaning and such like? All we had time to do was run, run, run. And hide and be scared and pray. But mostly just run. I made a mistake. Mama said I wasn't to leave her side no matter what. But I did. I was thirsty. That's what it was. I was thirsty until I thought I'd surely die if I didn't get a mouthful of water – and soon. And what made it worse was that in the distance I could see a well. It was just beyond the edge of some trees, not too far away from a main house. The house wasn't as grand as Best Friend's – I could see that much – but it was the well that had most of my attention. Mama was dozing – one of the few moments since we'd started running that I'd seen her take any kind of rest. I climbed down out of the tree, quiet as an ant with a secret, and headed for the well. I only had eyes for the well – and that was my mistake. I was close enough to almost smell the water in it, when all at once there came a yapping and howling and barking that sent my heart shooting up towards my ears and plunging back down to my toes. Three snarling, vicious dogs were tied to a fence ring – and in my haste to get some water, I hadn't even seen them. They howled at me, slathering and slobbering and I stared at them, my feet rooted to the ground. The front door of the main house opened. Two white men came out to see what all the dogs' fussing was about.

'You, child.'

I stared at them, realizing now just what I'd done.

'Yes, you, child. What're you doing there? Who are you?'

One of the men came down the house steps and started walking towards me.

Someone pulled at my arm, pulling me away from the man. Frantically, I turned, ready to lash out. It was Mama.

'Run, child. Run!'

Mama and I took off like the wind, darting in and out of the trees around us. I heard calling and shouting and the dogs bark, bark, barking like they were more than ready to tear us apart. Behind us, I heard a sudden yelp, then another and another, and knew that the dogs had been released and they were after us. And still Mama and I ran and ran.

The whole world was nothing but a long, hard road to run on. We ran for our lives. I wanted to stop and catch my breath. I wanted to pause and tell Mama I was sorry, but with the dogs chasing us I knew I couldn't. Mama didn't even look at me. She held my hand and pulled me after her as we tried to escape. The dogs behind us were getting closer. Abruptly, Mama stopped. There was no more solid ground. We were at the top of a waterfall with what seemed like a for ever long drop to the rushing river below.

And behind us, the dogs were getting closer.

'Mama . . .'

'Jump.'

I opened my mouth but I'll never know what I was going to say, because the next thing I knew we were falling, falling. I managed to let out a scream and then the icy water hit my whole body and filled my mouth. Down, down, down I went. But that wasn't what frightened me half to death. It was not feeling

Mama's hand holding mine. For the first time I felt alone. I opened my mouth to scream and swallowed half the river. And then I was being dragged up and dragged out. I vomited up everything in my stomach. I vomited until it felt like I was bringing up the first meal I'd ever had after being a baby. I coughed and spluttered and retched until my whole body shook like someone with the palsy.

'Come on, angel. We must keep going,' Mama panted, her sack still hitched high on one shoulder.

'No, Mama. I can't,' I managed to gasp out. 'I can't. I can't.'

'You must.'

But I wasn't moving. I had no strength to even get to my feet, never mind run. I shook my head, too bone-tired to even argue.

'Look, there's a hollow over there.' Mama pointed across the river a ways. 'It might be a cave. We'll stay there until you've got your strength back.'

Half staggering and with Mama half dragging me, we moved down river until it looked shallow enough to wade across. I couldn't hear dogs or men shouting or anything else. Just the river, rushing and roaring like it was mad at us for disturbing it. We finally made it across by jumping and wading. Then we climbed up a steep slope to the hollow Mama thought she'd seen. It was little more than a cut in the rock. It was set back some so that with luck, bad eyesight and darkness we might not be spotted, but I knew we couldn't rely on that. The wind was picking up now, like there was a storm coming. Mama sniffed at the air, then shook her head.

'I'll be all right in a minute, Mama,' I whispered. But it was a lie. I felt sick and was too weary to hide it.

Mama smiled and stroked my face, her callused fingers tender against my skin.

'We'll do fine, sugar,' she whispered back.

But then I heard the dogs. The barking was coming from in front of us. Behind us was the waterfall so we couldn't go back. And across the river was a steep, steep bank. The dogs would be on us before we were more than halfway up. And now I could hear the sound of dogs coming from behind us as well. And where

there were dogs there were owners and white men –
the brethren of Best Friend.

'We're not going to make it, are we, Mama?'

'It don't seem so.'

And those words were as heavy as the world, bend-
ing my head and breaking my back.

'Mama, don't let them take me back. I don't never
want to go back.'

'You ain't going back, my love. You're going
north.' Mama smiled.

'But we're surrounded. They'll take us back and
whip us and then Best Friend will sell me . . .'

The fear I felt was like heavy rocks piled up on top
of me. And there was no way out, no way away. I'd
seen what Best Friend and his foreman had done to
other slaves who dared to try and run away. They
were whipped until what little flesh there was left on
their backs hung like strips of meat in the smoke-
house. I couldn't stand that. I knew I couldn't.

'Mama—'

'Hush, child. Hush. You're going to be free. Didn't
I promise you?'

'But . . .'

'Lean against me and close your eyes.'

I looked at Mama. She had tears in her eyes but the smile she gave me lit my heart. I hugged her tight then turned to lie with my back against her chest.

'Close your eyes and see Heaven, my love,' Mama whispered.

I heard her fish in her sack. I knew what she was looking for. I smiled. And as my smile grew fatter, so my fear grew thinner until it was all but gone. I opened my eyes and saw Mama's knife in her hand. I closed my eyes again.

'I love you, angel,' Mama whispered in my ear.

'I'm going to be free.' I reached out my hands in front of me. I could see freedom, even though my eyes were closed. I could almost touch it. It was only seconds away. I felt nothing but pure, pure joy. Joy like nothing I'd ever felt before. Joy enough to fill the whole wide world. 'I'm going north, Mama. I'm going *north.*'

And Mama's knife moved against my throat.

LANGSTON HUGHES

Freedom

Freedom will not come
Today, this year
    Nor ever
Through compromise and fear.

I have as much right
As the other fellow has
    To stand
On my two feet
And own land.

I tire so of hearing people say,

Let things take their course.
Tomorrow is another day.
I do not need freedom when I am dead.
I cannot live on tomorrow's bread.

Freedom
Is a strong seed
Planted
In a great need.
I live here, too.
I want freedom
Just as you.

MARY PRINCE

Extracts from:

The History of Mary Prince,
a West Indian Slave

Mary Prince makes a plea against the inhumanity of slavery.

Oh the horrors of slavery! – How the thought of it pains my heart! But the truth ought to be told of it; and what my eyes have seen I think it is my duty to relate; for few people in England know what slavery is. I have been a slave – I have felt what a slave feels, and I know what a slave knows; and I would have all the good people in England to know it too, that they may break our chains, and set us free.

* * *

I still live in the hope that God will find a way to give me my liberty, and give me back to my husband. I endeavour to keep down my fretting, and to leave all to Him, for he knows what is good for me better than I know myself. Yet, I must confess, I find it a hard and heavy task to do so.

I am often much vexed, and I feel great sorrow when I hear some people in this country say, that the slaves do not need better usage, and do not want to be free. They believe the foreign people, who deceive them, and say slaves are happy. I say, Not so. How can slaves be happy when they have the halter round their neck and the whip upon their back? and are disgraced and thought no more of than beasts? – and are separated from their mothers, and husbands, and children, and sisters, just as cattle are sold and separated? Is it happiness for a driver in the field to take down his wife or sister or child, and strip them, and whip them in such a disgraceful manner? – women that have had children exposed in the open field to shame! There is no modesty or decency shown by the owner to his slaves; men, women, and children are exposed alike. Since I have been here I have often wondered how English people can go out into the West Indies and act in such a beastly manner. But when they go to the West Indies, they forget God and all feeling of shame, I think, since they can see and do such things. They tie up slaves like hogs – moor them up like cattle, and they lick them, so as hogs, or cattle, or horses never were flogged; – and yet they come home and say, and make some good people believe, that slaves don't want to get out of slavery. But they put a cloak about the truth. It is not so. All slaves want to be free – to be free is very sweet. I will say the truth to English people who may read this history that my good friend, Miss S——, is now writing down for me. I have been a slave myself – and I know what slaves feel – I can tell by myself what other slaves feel, and by what they have told me.

The man that says slaves be quite happy in slavery – that they don't want to be free – that man is either ignorant or a lying person. I never heard a slave so say. I never heard a Buckra man say so, till I heard tell of it in England. Such people ought to be ashamed of themselves. They can't do without slaves, they say. What's the reason they can't do without slaves as well as in England? No slaves here – no whips – no stocks – no punishment, except for wicked people. They hire servants in England, and if they don't like them, they send them away: they can't lick them. Let them work ever so hard in England, they are far better off than slaves. If they get a bad master, they give warning and go hire to another. They have their liberty. That's just what we want. We don't mind hard work, if we had proper treatment, and proper wages like English servants, and proper time given in the week to keep us from breaking the Sabbath. But they won't give it: they will have work – work – work, night and day, sick or well, till we are quite done up; and we must not speak up nor look amiss, however much we be abused. And then when we are quite done up, who cares for us, more than for a lame horse? This is slavery. I tell it, to let English people know the truth; and I hope they will never leave off to pray God, and call loud to the great King of England, till all the poor blacks be given free, and slavery done up for evermore.

PART FIVE

THE LEGACY OF SLAVERY

BENJAMIN ZEPHANIAH

Master, Master

Master master drank a toast
And dreamt of easy tea,
He gave to you a Holy Ghost,
    Come children see.

From Liverpool on sinking ships
Blessed by a monarchy,
To Africa the hypocrites,
    Come children see.

Master master worked the slave
Who ran for liberty,

The master made us perm and shave,
  Come children see.

If slave drivers be men of words
We curse that poetry,
Its roots you'll find are so absurd,
  Come children see.

Master master's sons drill oil
It's all his legacy,
They put the devil in the soil,
  Come children see.

Fear not his science or his gun
Just know what you can be,
And children we shall overcome,
  Come children see.

Tis true that we have not now chains
Yet we were never free,
Still master's chains corrupt our brains,
  Come children see.

A word is slave for man is man
What's done is slavery,
The evils of the clan that can,
    Come children see.

Master master worked the slave
The upright sort was he,
That boy dug master master's grave
    Come children see.

Some now await a judgement day
To know his penalty,
It's blood and fire anyway,
    Come children see.

GRACE QUANSAH

The Awakening of Elmina

I remember when my family of ten
Took a trip from England
To our ancestral land of Ghana,
For the purpose of baptising
My baby daughter,
In the Western region
Of coastal Nzema.

On route from the capital of Accra
In a bus on private hire,
We decided to stop off in Elmina
To visit its castle, which seemed to play host
To our arrival.

As I walked towards the white foreboding building
That once kept thousands of Ghanaians captive,
Whilst hearing the waves whipping the rocks nearby,
I pondered to myself, 'Why oh why
Did so many of my people have to suffer and die?'

Two of my sons posed for a photo
Right next to a row of grotesque-looking cannons
That had somehow now become a tourist attraction.
Still, for me, there was no satisfaction,
As it seemed that deep within my veins,
My blood was boiling,
For this castle was a symbol of pain.

A guide invited us inside to survey its contents,
Of this so-called 'World Heritage Monument',
But once I ventured through the iron gate,
I could not wait to make my exit.
I pondered silently again,
'How could anyone exist like this
With conditions so inhumane?'

Built by the Portuguese in 1482
As a trading post for goods and provisions,
Elmina became strategic for human cargo,
So much so that its storerooms became dungeons,
To imprison thousands upon thousands of Africans.

These cave-like rooms were a grim reminder
Of how our ancestors had passed to their doom.
For those who survived,
The legacy of slavery continued to loom,
As many descendants in the Diaspora
Were forced to break with African culture
In all sorts of ways to the present day.

When my family of ten left Elmina,
We brought back with us lasting memories
Of a painful history.
For never would we forget
The abhorrent atrocities our ancestors met.
And always would we remember with pride,
In spite of the African genocide,
That our cultural legacies positively exist for ever.

Elmina Castle is now an official World Heritage Site in Ghana. The castle was built by the Portuguese in 1482, originally as a trading post for goods. However, as the demand for slaves increased, the castle storerooms were converted into dungeons and, over close to the next 300 years, hundreds of thousands of captives were incarcerated there before being shipped off to the Americas and the Caribbean.

JAMES BERRY

The poet describes what influenced him to write the poem 'Letter to Mother Africa'

From about eight or nine years old I began to notice how the ex-slave-owners' descendants of my village treated my father automatically as an inferior. And my father accepted his position, as if it was all in the way of things. A terror settled in me that I was placed to grow up into my father's position. Inward, thoughtful, anxious, desperate to read books nobody had, I lived with the dread that lack of money and education and opportunity would condemn me to repeat that same design of life impressed upon my ancestors up to my father.

Shelley's line 'I fall upon the thorns of life! I

bleed!' could describe the silent state of mind in a continuing pain that gathered itself and became 'Letter to Mother Africa'.

I had seen and understood that nobody liked Africa. Yet, it was much later I realised I knew and understood nothing positive about Africa and Africans. At school Africa embarrassed us and stirred us with a sense of shame, like slavery did. Our feelings for Africa aroused more horror and dread and hatred than any curiosity.

An impelling need grew in me. Mentally, I needed to go back to my African roots with my hurt, anger and a complaining voice. My state of mind became fixed on addressing my ancestral country, continent and rulership, as to a child-abandoning mother.

Equality meant shouldering a share of responsibility. I wanted Mother Africa to voice acknowledging a share of responsibility for the under-human and outsider status that was allowed to be implanted into the life and being of African descendants in Western society.

In Our Year 1941 My Letter to You Mother Africa

I sit

under the mango tree in our yard.

A woman passes along the village road,

loaded like a donkey.

                    I remember

I start my seventeenth year today

full of myself, but worried, and sad

remembering, you sold my ancestors

labelled, *not for human rights*,

And, O, your non-rights terms were

the fire of hell that stuck.

                    Mother Africa

my space walks your face

and I am condemned.

I refuse to grow up fixed here

going on with plantation lacks

and that lack of selfhood. Easily

I could grow up all drastic and extreme

and be wasted by law.
I want a university in me as I grow.

    And now
      three village men pass together,
        each gripping his plantation machete.
            I remember
we are stuck in time and hidden.
I refuse to be stuck in a maze
gripping a plantation machete.
I refuse to be Estate 'chop-bush' man
and a poverty path scarecrow.
Refuse to live in the terror of floods
and drought, and live left-out and moneyless.
I refuse to worry-worry Jesus Christ
with tear-faced complaints. And, O, I refuse
to walk my father's deadness,
Schooled to be wasted lawfully

and refuse it
I am doubly doomed to be wasted by law,
                    Mother Africa
New World offices and yards of rejection
threaten me, like every shack dweller seared
by poverty and feels disgraced.
And people positioned to make changes
are not bothered how poverty sinks in.
Help stop my vexed feelings growing.
Help me have a university in me.

    And now
      a banana-truck passes.
            I remember
I dread that cap-in-hand
my father. His selfhood gutted –
all seasoned plantation corned-pork –
no education habit is there.
Not seeing his need and his rights
to help make the world free,
not seeing the club of countries
that confiscated his ancestors' lives

still set his boundaries, not seeing
no god for our good with us,
my father demands no more
than a small cut of land, hidden.
                              Mother Africa
nobody at home here has any
education habit. Nobody stirs differently.
And I want life of the world in print.
I want to move about in all ages.
Not stay deformed, arrested, driven
by any drillmaster's voice telling
the growing good of myself is cancelled.
I want to be healed of smashed-up selfhood,
healed of the beating-up by bad-man history.
I want a university in me as a man.

   And now
   children pass by, going to loiter
   around the tourist beach.
                        I remember
you were pillaged easily
and gutted easily. Existing dumb

you lost your continental wealth,
our inheritance, my inheritance.
And, a settled absence, you are a fixed
nonparticipator I never see. And while
others come and go from their motherlands,
I live marooned, renamed 'Negro'
meaning, of no origin,
not eligible for human rights.

                        Mother Africa
I walk your face
and my heritage is pain.
And there somewhere
you make not one move.
Say nothing. Do nothing.
And I feel excessive doings could grip me.
I could call on bad doings as normal
and be wasted by law.
I want a university in me.

    And now
    at our gate, a village beggar stands
    calling my mother.

I remember
I am third generation since slavery,
born into people stricken in traps,
Eight generations departed
with a last sigh, aware they leave
offsprings all heirs to losses,
to nothing, to a shame, and to faces
who meet enmity in the offices
of their land and the world.
You say nothing, do nothing
while your bosom's gold and gems are stars
in other people's days
around the world. And scattered
stubbornly, we are here
in the sun's comings and goings
anguished for our human status back.
Mother Africa
do you know, cruelties of your lacks
join forces with New World mangling?
Now I want to be healed.
I want university.

And now
village voices go by
strong with the adjective 'black'
in their curses.
                    I remember
in lessons at school you were degraded.
No village man accepts his photographs
that printed him truly black.
You never made a contact
never inspired me
never nurtured, counselled or consoled me.
I have never seen you, Africa,
never seen your sights or heard your sounds,
never heard your voice at home,
never understood one common
family thing about you beneath
one crinkly head or naked breast.
Any wonder I have no love for you?
Any wonder everybody at school despised
you?
Tradition has it, our people's travel
to you does not happen. Visits

to a motherland are overlords' privilege.
What is your privilege?

                    Mother Africa
I want university.
Is there any help in you?
Will I have to store,
or bag-up and walk with, inherited hurt
and outrage of enslavement?
Will I transcend it?
Or will I grow up wasted
in deformity or being outlaw?

HISTORICAL NOTE

The trade in African slaves began more than 500 years ago. African men, women and children were captured by slave traders and transported to colonies in the Caribbean, Central and South America, Europe and North America.

The trade rapidly escalated during the sixteenth and seventeenth centuries. Many slaves were owned by plantation owners who lived in Britain, and by the early 1700s Britain had become the principal slave-trading nation. The trade reached its peak in the 1780s, with a new slave ship leaving Britain every two days.

Conditions on the slave ships were appallingly brutal, overcrowded and unhygienic, and many slaves died onboard from sickness or starvation. Only the most resilient survived. Some were killed for attempting escape or for simply not being strong and healthy enough.

A typical Atlantic crossing took 60–90 days but could last up to four months. Once they had arrived at their destination, captains sold the surviving slaves and used the money to purchase goods to take back on their return journey. Roughly 54,000 voyages were made by Europeans to buy and sell slaves.

The full extent of the human cost of the slave trade is impossible to quantify. It is estimated that around 24 million people were enslaved while the transatlantic slave trade was in force. At least two thirds – approximately 16 million – died within three years of their enslavement, even if they managed to survive the gruelling journey.

Treated as mere commodities, most of the slaves laboured on plantations or farms, or in mines. The working conditions were harsh, often horrific, and slaves were at the mercy of their master.

By 1783 an anti-slavery movement was beginning among the British public. Olaudah Equiano's autobiography became a bestseller in 1789 and was published in nine editions in his lifetime. He travelled extensively to promote the book, and his anti-slavery message reached far and wide. Frederick Douglass also played a large part in spreading the abolitionist message.

William Wilberforce became the parliamentary spokesman for the abolition of the slave trade, and he campaigned tirelessly despite initial fierce opposition.

On 25 March 1807 the British Parliament passed the Abolition of the Slave Trade Act, under which captains of slave ships could be fined £100 for each slave found on board a British ship. But it was only in 1833 that all slaves in the British empire were freed, with the Slavery Abolition Act.

Here is a timeline of some of the key dates in the history of slavery:

1444 The first sale of slaves to the public, in Portugal

1518 The first known shipment of slaves direct from Africa to the Americas

1630s More and more plantations are set up in the Americas, and British interest in the slave trade is increased, with several companies set up specifically to deal with it

1700s Britain becomes the world's most dominant slave-trading nation

1807 The Abolition of the Slave Trade Act outlaws the trade in slaves on British ships across the Atlantic

1808 The United States passes laws to ban the slave trade

1811 Slavery is abolished in Spain and the Spanish
colonies (except for Cuba)

1813 Sweden bans slave trading

1814 The Netherlands bans slave trading

1817 France bans slave trading, effective from
1826

1823 The Anti-Slavery Society is formed in Britain

1833 The Abolition of Slavery Act is passed, which
slowly abolishes slavery in the British empire

1848 Slavery is abolished in France

1858 Slavery is abolished in Portugal and in its
colonies

1861 Slavery is abolished in the Dutch colonies in
the Caribbean area

1865 Slavery is abolished in the USA, following
the Civil War

1886 Slavery is abolished in Cuba

1888 Slavery is abolished in Brazil

Sadly, slavery is still present in many countries in the world today.

For further information:
  www.antislavery.org.uk
  www.black-history-month.co.uk
  www.amnesty.org

NOTES ON CONTRIBUTORS

MALORIE BLACKMAN, the editor of the collection, is acknowledged as one of today's most imaginative and convincing writers for young readers. Her books for Random House Children's Books include the award-winning *Noughts & Crosses* trilogy (the first of which won the Children's Book Award, the Sheffield Children's Book Award and the Lancashire Children's Book Award), *Hacker*, *Thief!*, *A.N.T.I.D.O.T.E.*, *Dangerous Reality*, *Dead Gorgeous* and *Pig-Heart Boy* (which was shortlisted for the Carnegie Medal and adapted into a BAFTA-award-winning TV serial). Both *Hacker* and *Thief!* won the Young Telegraph/Gimme 5 Award – Malorie is the only author to have won this twice – and *Hacker* also won the W H Smith Mind-Boggling Books Award. In 2005 Malorie was honoured with the Eleanor Farjeon Award in recognition of her distinguished contribution to the world of children's books. She lives with her husband and daughter in Kent.

JOHN AGARD was born in Guyana and came to Britain in 1977. His poetry has been published for over thirty years, he has performed on television and around the world and is a popular children's writer whose titles include *We Animals Would Like a Word with You*, which won a Smarties Award. He also won the Casa de las Americas Poetry Prize in 1982 for *Man to Pan*, has won the Guyana Prize twice, was the first Writer in Residence at London's South Bank Centre in 1993 and was awarded the CLPE Poetry Award in 2003 for *Under the Moon and Over the Sea*, a poetry collection co-edited with his partner Grace Nichols. He has extensively promoted Caribbean culture and poetry as a touring speaker with the Commonwealth Institute and was Writer in Residence for the BBC in 1998 with the Windrush Project. He lives in Sussex.

SANDRA AGARD was born in Hackney to Guyanese parents and is a writer and storyteller. Her repertoire includes stories from all over the world. She runs regular storytelling, creative writing and reading development sessions in the community. Her poetry and short stories has been published in *A Girl's Best Friend* and *Watchers and Seekers*; *Tales, Myths and Legends* and *Time for Telling*. She has also written plays. She has a particular love for tales from an African, African-American and Caribbean background as well as Black British oral history projects. She still lives in East London and works as a Literature Development Officer in South London at Peckham and New Cross Libraries.

JAMES BERRY was born and raised in Jamaica, but now lives in England. In 1982 he won the National Poetry Society's Annual Prize for *Fantasy of an African Boy*, and his collection of short stories for young readers, *A Thief in the Village*, was the Grand Prix winner of the Smarties Prize in 1987. *Ajeemah and His Son* was the winner of a 1993 Boston Globe-Horn Book Award and in 1990 he was awarded an OBE in recognition of his contribution to people of all ages through his writing.

FREDERICK DOUGLASS: see page 53.

OLAUDAH EQUIANO: see page 134.

DANIEL ALOYSIUS FRANCIS was born in Castries, St Lucia, and moved to London when he was four. He therefore has first-hand experience of the different cultures that are at the heart of his writing. Daniel was inspired to write the poem 'A Day in the Life' by images exploring the relationship between slavery and religion. He also drew on the work of Braithwaite and Afrika, which he is studying as part of his GCSE in English. He lives in London.

ALEX HALEY, a black American, taught himself to write during a twenty-year career in the US Coast Guard. He became its first Chief Journalist, a position he held until he retired in 1959 to become a magazine writer and interviewer. His first book was *The Autobiography of Malcolm X*, published in 1965, after which he spent twelve years researching and writing *Roots*, which became a publishing phenomenon and international bestseller and was adapted for television in 1977, attracting over 130 million viewers. In it, Haley traced his ancestry back to Africa and covered seven generations, starting with his ancestor Kunta Kinte. He died in 1992.

LANGSTON HUGHES was born in 1902 and grew up in Kansas, USA, publishing his first poems whilst still in high school, with his famous poem 'The Negro Speaks of Rivers' appearing in 1921, when he was only nineteen years old. He published his first collection in 1926 and further poetry, novels, plays, short stories and essays over the next forty-six years. He travelled widely throughout his life, both in the US and abroad: he visited the Soviet Union in the 1930s, and Europe in 1937 to cover the Spanish Civil War as a journalist. He died in 1967.

HARRIET JACOBS: see page 90.

CATHERINE JOHNSON was born and still lives in London. Her father is from Jamaica and her mother is Welsh; both were good storytellers. She studied art and film at St Martin's School of Art and has now written nine novels for young adults, including *Face Value*, and *The Dying Game*, as well as a number of scripts for the screen, most recently for the award-winning film *Bullet Boy*. She also mentors writers all over Africa for the British Council and has run writing groups for teenagers in London, as well as doing school visits and running creative writing workshops.

GRACE NICHOLS was born in Guyana and grew up in a small country village on the coast. She worked as a teacher and journalist, before moving to the UK in 1977. Her first poetry collection, *I Is a Long Memoried Woman*, won the Commonwealth Poetry Prize in 1983, and a subsequent film adaptation of the book was awarded a gold medal at the International Film and Television Festival of New York. She was also awarded the CLPE Poetry Award in 2003 for *Under the Moon and Over the Sea*, a poetry collection co-edited with her partner, John Agard. She lives in Sussex.

GARY PAULSEN grew up in the Philippines and has worked as a sailor, archer, trapper, singer, actor and carnival worker. He is the distinguished author of many critically acclaimed books for young readers – over 175 titles and some 200 articles and short stories for young readers and adults – including three Newbery Honor books, *The Winter Room*, *Hatchet* and *Dogsong*. His books, *The Beet Fields* and *How Angel Peterson Got His*

Name, are both published on the Random House lists. He lives in New Mexico and on a boat in the Pacific, with his wife, the painter Ruth Wright Paulsen.

MARY PRINCE: see page 60.

GRACE QUANSAH ('Akuba'), of Ghanaian descent, was born and reared in London. Having lectured in several academic institutions since 1988, including The Open University, she currently works as a freelance facilitator at the British Museum. She also enjoys writing and performing poetry and African-centred folktales. Her poems, *Hungry For Mother's Love*, *Mothering Lasts Forever*, *Is There Safety in Self-Denial*, and *Sexual Emotion* are to be published in a second anthology by Shangwe, 2007. A visit to the Castle of Elmina during a recent trip to Ghana with her four children inspired her poem. She lives in London.

LALITA TADEMY was born in California. She pursued a very successful business career over a period of twenty years, but resigned as vice-president of a technology company in Silicon Valley when she discovered her great-great-great-great-grandmother's original Bill of Sale and began to research her family history. *Cane River* was the result − a novel based on the lives of four generations of Creole slave women in Louisiana, the women from whom she was descended.

BENJAMIN ZEPHANIAH was born in Birmingham. He is one of Britain's best-known poets, variously called a dub poet, an oral poet, a performance poet, a pop poet, a rap poet, a Rasta poet, a reggae poet . . . but says that if he had to choose one he would start with 'oral poet' as he can 'hear the sound of it' as he writes his poetry. As an oral poet, with a strong commitment to social justice, he puts his poetry into music and plays, performs on television and radio, records his poetry to music and as spoken word cassettes − and is also published in many books and anthologies, such as *Talking Turkeys* and, more recently, *We Are Britain* and *Too Black, Too Strong*. He has also written a number of novels for young readers, including *Refugee Boy* and *Gangsta Rap*.

ACKNOWLEDGEMENTS

Random House Children's Books are grateful for permission to include the following copyright material in this anthology:

John Agard, 'Newton's Amazing Grace' from *We Brits* (Bloodaxe Books, 2006). Copyright © John Agard, 2006. Reprinted by permission of Bloodaxe Books.

Sandra Agard, 'Runaway' (Random House Children's Books, 2007). Copyright © Sandra Agard, 2007.

James Berry, extract from 'Ajeemah and His Son' from *The Future-Telling Lady* (Hamish Hamilton, 1991). Copyright © James Berry, 1991. Reprinted by permission of PFD on behalf of James Berry. 'In Our Year 1941 a Letter to You Mother Africa' and extract from the preface to *Hot Earth Cold Earth* (Bloodaxe Books, 1995). Copyright © James Berry, 1995. Reprinted by permission of Bloodaxe Books.

Malorie Blackman, 'North' (Random House Children's Books, 2007). Copyright © Malorie Blackman, 2007.

Frederick Douglass, extract from *The Narrative of the Life of Frederick Douglass, an American Slave* is reprinted from the 1845 edition, published by the Anti-Slavery Office in Boston, as it appears in *The Classic Slave Narratives*, edited by Henry Louis Gater, Jr (Signet Classic, 1987).

Olaudah Equiano, extract from *The Interesting Narrative of the Life of Olaudah Equiano, or Gustavus Vassa* is reprinted from the 1814 edition, published in Leeds by J. Nichols, as it appears in *The Classic Slave Narratives*, edited by Henry Louis Gater, Jr (Signet Classic, 1987).

Daniel Aloysius Francis, 'A Day in the Life' (Random House Children's Books, 2007). Copyright © Daniel Aloysius Francis, 2007.

Alex Haley, extract from *Roots* (Hutchinson, 1977). Copyright © Alex Haley, 1976. Reprinted by permission of The Random House Group Ltd.

THE STUFF OF NIGHTMARES
by Malorie Blackman

It begins with a ride on a train.

But where it ends is on a precipice of horror –
dangling on the border between life and death.

It's a moment when Kyle discovers that he's not the
only one in his class who knows about fear.

Not the only one who has nightmares.

And now, as Death stalks the carriages, it's a moment
when nightmares become real. Nightmares of wars, of
a body being slowly stolen, bit by bit. Of monstrous
actions and monstrous creatures from old myths.
Of jealousy, obsession and a stalker outside your
window. Nightmares of everything imaginable.

What will it take for Kyle to finally face *his*
greatest fear?

A seriously creepy new novel from award-winning
Malorie Blackman, available in Doubleday hardback
from September 2007.

978 0 385 61043 8

NOUGHTS & CROSSES

by Malorie Blackman

Callum is a nought – a second-class citizen in a world run by the ruling Crosses . . .

Sephy is a Cross, daughter of one of the most power-ful men in the country . . .

In their world, noughts and Crosses simply don't mix. And as hostility turns to violence, can Callum and Sephy possibly find a way to be together?

They are determined to try.

And then the bomb explodes . . .

A gripping and totally absorbing novel set in a world where black and white are right and wrong – the first book in the acclaimed Noughts & Crosses Trilogy.

A special new edition includes *An Eye for An Eye*, a stunning novella that continues the tale told in *Noughts & Crosses*.

978 0 552 55570 8

KNIFE EDGE

by Malorie Blackman

A frightened girl running barefoot on a knife edge . . .

That's how eighteen-year-old Sephy feels as she gazes down at her new-born daughter, Callie Rose. Whilst Sephy is a Cross, the baby's father, Callum, was a nought, giving Callie Rose dual heritage in a society where the ruling Crosses treat the pale-skinned noughts – blankers – as second-class citizens.

What kind of world will her daughter grow up into? One which is more equal? Or one where discrimination still has the power to destroy lives?

Sephy can only hope that the tomorrows will be better than the yesterdays. But Jude, Callum's brother is determined to have his revenge on both Sephy and her daughter. And he will make sure nothing stands in his way.

Sequel to the award-winning *Noughts & Crosses*, *Knife Edge* is a razor-sharp and intensely moving novel for older readers.

978 0 552 54892 2

CHECKMATE

by Malorie Blackman

Can the future ever erase the past?

Callie Rose has a Cross mother and a nought father
in a society where the pale-skinned noughts are
treated as inferiors and those with dual heritage face
a life-long battle against deep-rooted prejudices.

Sephy, her mother, has told Rose virtually nothing
about her father, raising her child alone while strug-
gling to make a living as a singer/songwriter. But as
Rose grows into a young adult, she unexpectedly discovers the truth about her parentage, with potentially
devastating results.

A dramatic and intensely moving novel, the third
in the award-winning *Noughts & Crosses* trilogy.

978 0 552 55194 6

PIG-HEART BOY

by Malorie Blackman

I am drowning in this roaring silence. I am drowning. I'm going to die . . .

Cameron is thirteen and desperately in need of a heart transplant when a pioneering doctor approaches his family with a startling proposal. He can give Cameron a new heart – but not from a human, one from a pig.

It's never been done before. It's experimental, risky and very controversial. But Cameron is fed up with just sitting on the side of life, always watching and never doing. He has to try – to become the world's first pig-heart boy.

'A powerful story . . . topical and controversial'
Guardian

'Blackman is becoming a bit of a national treasure'
The Times

'Few writers can sustain a plot as well as Malorie Blackman'
Sunday Telegraph

SHORTLISTED FOR THE CARNEGIE MEDAL
A BAFTA AWARD-WINNING TV SERIAL

978 0 552 55166 3

THE LAST TABOO
by Bali Rai

'Tyrone leaned across the table and gave me a long kiss. When I eventually opened my eyes I saw an Asian couple, middle-aged, on the next table along. You know that phrase – if looks could kill? Well, I was dead.'

Simran falls for Tyrone the moment she spots him in the crowd. He's gorgeous. Even better, he fancies her back. But there's one big problem: Tyrone is black.

It's the last taboo for an Asian girl – and one that others will do anything to enforce . . .

Also by the multi award-winning author Bali Rai:

(un)arranged marriage – 'Absorbing' *Observer*

The Crew – 'A jewel of a book' *Independent*

Rani & Sukh – 'Overwhelmingly powerful' *The Bookseller*

The Whisper – 'Energy and verbal brilliance evident on every page' *TES*

A hard-hitting novel about two teenagers facing up to the consequences of racial prejudice between Asian and Black communities, from award-winning author Bali Rai.

978 0 552 553 1 8